GOODBYE FOREVER

It was strange, wonderfully strange, to be with Noah. He made me laugh about things that had driven me to tears not too long ago.

Slowly, I slipped into a daydream. Noah and I were driving up the California coast. Suddenly, when we turned a bend, there was the most perfect beach in the world. With only one glance, we both knew we had to stop and take a swim. We jumped out of the car and raced toward the cool water. . . .

Then it hit me. Noah wasn't going to be in California. We'd have seven short days together, and then he'd go back to Pennsylvania. I'd let myself care for him, and once more, I'd be abandoned. Well, I wasn't going to let it happen again. "I've got to get back to my cabin, Noah," I said abruptly, and turned to leave.

Goodbye Forever

Barbara Conklin

BANTAM BOOKS
TORONTO • NEW YORK • LONDON • SYDNEY • AUCKLAND

RL 5, IL age 11 and up

GOODBYE FOREVER
A Bantam Book / November 1984

Cover photo by Pat Hill

ISBN 0-553-24356-X

Published simultaneously in the United States and Canada

Printed and bound in Great Britain by Hunt Barnard Printing Ltd.

O   0 9 8 7 6 5 4 3 2 1

To the S.S. Norway, may she grace the seas with her beauty for many years to come, and to my loyal readers, may you someday see your ships come in.

Chapter One

I was sad as I sat in the backseat of the car, my mother beside me. Aunt Camille relaxed in the front seat, watching the speedometer as Uncle Craig drove us home. Suddenly she twisted around to face my mother. "It was a beautiful wedding, Judith. Lisa looked gorgeous. And the gown you made her was spectacular."

She chatted on happily about the wedding and reception, her feelings so different from mine. For me it meant my sister wouldn't be coming home to share our room ever again—no more secrets whispered at night, no more silly jokes told in the morning. I was sure nothing could ever fill the hole she had left in my life. Yes, it had been a beautiful wedding, but I had cried all the way through it. I would miss Lisa so much.

1

I thought again of how she had looked. She had decided to wear her light blond hair down, not all piled up the way the hair stylist had wanted. It curled softly around her face, resting gently on her shoulders. It was perfect with her veil and crown of tiny pearls. She had used just the right touch of make-up: a blue eye shadow to bring out her gorgeous blue eyes, and pale red lipstick and a delicate blush. I'd watched and remembered it all. Lisa and I look alike, with the same blond hair and blue eyes, so now I'd know just how I wanted to look for a special occasion.

Of course, I'd never have such a stunning gown until I got married myself. It was our mother's own creation, a romantic ball gown with a billowing skirt, narrow waist, pouf sleeves and flowing train. I remembered helping Lisa into it, the taffeta fabric whispering as I buttoned the tiny pearl buttons up the back. Lisa had been the most elegant bride I'd ever seen. She was truly a rare beauty.

And I remembered Lisa's words to me as we waited in the room before the ceremony. It was our last one-to-one conversation. In a little while, Lisa would have someone else. And I'd be all alone.

"Oh, Kari, you look so sad," Lisa had said

in a whisper. "Aren't you happy for me on my wedding day?" She came over and sat down beside me, her gown flowing around her.

"Yes, I'm happy for you," I said, my eyes filling with tears. "Oh, darn! I'll have to redo my mascara."

Lisa smiled with understanding and reached over to clasp my hand. "I'm not going that far away," she said. "Just up to Berkeley. In less than a month, we'll be back down here for Christmas. And it's close enough for you to come and visit us often. Have you thought about that?"

"But you'll never live here again," I cried, my tears flowing freely now. I didn't really care what happened to my mascara now.

"Oh, you're like Mom." Lisa laughed softly and squeezed my shoulders. "Mom hates changes. She wishes we'd both stay little and never grow up. Well, she'll get used to it. I've already left home, and before you know it, it will be your turn. Things are different when you reach sixteen! Wonderfully different. Kari, you won't be lonely without me because boys are going to be knocking down the door to date you."

"No," I told her, quickly wiping away my tears. "You've left me alone in our room, and

3

I'll never find anyone to love me. And if I do, he'll probably leave one day, the same way you did."

"Silly Kari." Lisa hugged me and smiled. "In a few years, maybe less, on one of my visits here, you'll call me up to that room, which will be all yours to decorate for once, and tell me about a marvelous boy. You'll tell me he's crazy about you and you're crazy about him. You are lovely, Kari, but you haven't realized it yet."

In spite of myself, I grinned at my sister. Lisa pulled me close to her—well, as close as she could get with her puffy dress—and gave me a quick kiss on my wet cheek. She took a white lace hankie and carefully dried my tears. That only made me feel more alone. Without Lisa, who would wipe my tears away?

One hour later I was walking down the aisle in front of her as her maid of honor. I knew I looked elegant in my long gold gown, but not nearly so graceful as Lisa. I reached the spot where I was supposed to stand, and I turned to watch my beautiful sister walk down the aisle with Uncle Craig. All I could think was that it should have been Dad there, not Uncle Craig.

That thought returned to me now in the darkened car. I had been crushed by my

4

father's death two years earlier. Having Lisa to cry with had made it easier, but just as I was recovering from my loss, she had left. Couldn't I count on anyone I loved to stay with me? My mother leaned over and interrupted my unhappy thoughts. "Kari, are you OK?"

"Sure," I lied. "I'm fine. Tired, that's all."

"Yes, it has been a long day," she said, then sighed.

Aunt Camille turned around again and grinned at both of us. "But the day's not over!" She poked playfully at my uncle. "Craig and I have a surprise for you two. We're going to give it to you as soon as we reach the house."

I glanced at my mother, and from the look on her face, I knew she was just as puzzled as I was. "I don't think I can stand much more today, Camille," my mother told her sister. "I've been on my feet since four-thirty this morning, putting finishing touches on the gown and checking on the hundreds of last-minute details. All I want to do now is go home and go to bed."

Aunt Camille turned and smiled at us again. "You can go to bed if you want," she said, grinning from ear to ear, "but after our surprise, I doubt very much if either one of you will be able to sleep!"

*　*　*

My mother looked down at the large manila envelope Aunt Camille had handed her. "I'm almost afraid to open it. If it's as exciting as you say, I won't be able to handle it."

Aunt Camille laughed. "Go ahead, Judith. I can't stand the suspense another minute."

My mother reached into the envelope. Slowly she pulled out an aqua-colored folder. In large letters on the front it said, "S.S. *Norway*—Let Yourself Go."

I looked over at my aunt and uncle. "What's the S.S. *Norway*?"

My mother paused for a moment, and then carefully she pulled out two tickets. "NCL," she read. "Norwegian Caribbean Lines." Her face flushed with excitement, she looked over at Aunt Camille. "Camille, a cruise for two! What does this mean?"

"It's a gift to you and Kari—also, we're throwing in the plane tickets to Miami," Aunt Camille said, putting her arms around my mother. "It's to thank you for all the time you spent with me after my operation last winter. A hired nurse would never have given me the long, tender hours you did. So this is for all the love and attention you both showered on

6

me and for all the times you had a hot dinner waiting for Craig."

"But, Camille, Craig, we can't accept this," my mother said softly. "It's just too extravagant. Why don't you two go?"

"No," my aunt said with certainty, "Craig would be miserable. He gets seasick just watching "Love Boat" on TV."

"But I can't take off from my job," my mother persisted. "And Kari has school."

"Ah-ha!" my uncle piped up. "We took care of that. The trip is only seven days long. Camille talked to Dr. Lampson, and he said he could get along with a replacement for that short amount of time."

"But Kari—"

"We checked on that, too," Uncle Craig went on. She'll miss only a few days of school because of Christmas vacation. We got proper permission from the principal, who was very helpful."

My mother sighed and pushed her dark brown hair out of her eyes. "Oh, you two!" she exclaimed, smiling at my aunt and uncle. "When you've decided something is going to be done your way, it gets done your way. So what do we wear on this cruise?"

I let out a whoop. "Hurray, you mean we can go?" I cried.

"Why not?" Mom laughed and hugged her sister.

Later that night, as I changed into my pajamas, I thought of that warm, loving hug. Time and distance certainly hadn't made Mom and Aunt Camille any less close. Still, it was strange to look across the room and see Lisa's empty bed. Carefully I hung my gown in the closet. I could shorten it a little and remove some of the fancy lace, and it would be perfect for the few formal occasions on the cruise.

There came a gentle knock on my door, and Aunt Camille poked her head into the room. I could hear Mom and Uncle Craig still talking and laughing downstairs. "May I come in?" my aunt asked.

"Oh, sure," I said and smiled. "You were right about being too excited to go to sleep. I'd love some company. This room feels empty without Lisa." I jumped upon my bed and pulled the blanket up over my knees.

"So you finally have it all to yourself." Aunt Camille smiled gently as she glanced around. "I've always wanted a room to myself.

But, as you know, I had to share one with your mother, and since I left home first, I never got my own room. Now I share one with your Uncle Craig." She laughed.

"I never wanted my own room," I told her. "I'd rather have Lisa."

My aunt slowly shook her head. "Oh, dear Kari, you'll get used to it."

"No, I won't," I said softly.

"But in just a few years, you will fall in love, too," my aunt said as she sat on the edge of my bed.

"I don't think there will ever be a boy for me," I told her.

She threw her head back and laughed again. After a moment she turned to me, her expression serious. "Kari, someday when you least expect it, you'll find your prince. You'll turn a corner, and there he'll be. And you won't even suspect it until you turn the bend."

"But, Aunt Camille," I cried, "I don't even want that prince. Having a boyfriend usually means breaking up at some point. And losing Lisa has been bad enough. I don't ever want to love anyone if it means having to go through this unhappiness again." The words poured out in a rush of honesty. Once they were out, I knew they expressed my fears completely.

Aunt Camille sighed. "Kari, I understand how you feel. After all, I had to leave your mother when we were girls ourselves, and we really missed each other. We still do when things get busy and we don't see each other as often as usual." She smiled. "But we continue to have good times together and to share special thoughts and feelings. Lisa isn't gone forever, and in a week or two, you won't miss her so terribly."

"I don't know about that," I said.

"Trust me. And as for that prince, who you will meet sometime soon, when you do have to leave him, you'll have many wonderful memories to keep you company. So don't worry about it." She leaned over and gave me a little kiss. "Now, don't think about it anymore and go to sleep." She stood up and crossed to the door, saying, "That is, if you can, with this cruise coming up. You know, it's going to be a real adventure, so exciting and romantic. Just about anything can happen!" And with that Aunt Camille flicked off my light and walked out, leaving me alone in my own room.

Chapter Two

"Miami! There are no words for it!" It was the morning of the day we'd be sailing on the S.S. *Norway*, and my mother was standing at the hotel window, peering through her binoculars excitedly.

"Get yourself out of that bed!" she commanded. "I think our ship's coming into the harbor right now." I knew she would give me no peace until I joined her at the window.

Slowly, and with much yawning, I pulled on my robe and went over to where my mother stood. It was only six-thirty. Mom had insisted on getting up that early so we could explore Miami. When the alarm clock buzzed, all I'd wanted to do was get back under the covers. Now, I stood with my eyes wide open, taking in the Miami skyline.

And there it was, a blue-and-white dream

of a ship, sailing gracefully into the port. The S.S. *Norway.*

The brochure said the ship completed a round trip every Saturday, so it was just coming in from a cruise now. The passengers would leave, then the crew would scurry around madly and ready it for a new group of passengers, much like a hotel staff cleans and polishes a room for a new guest. Except this was on a much larger scale. The S.S. *Norway* held almost twenty-eight hundred crew members and passengers combined. It was the largest cruise ship in the world, and from where we stood, it was easy to believe.

Two huge blue-and-white smokestacks towered majestically seventeen stories above the sea. The morning sun touched the portholes, making them look like a golden necklace draped around the ship. The ship's decks were alive with people saying farewell to the crew and their glamorous home for the past week. I could imagine their mixture of happiness and sadness. Goodbyes were hard. I knew that from experience. I tried to push the thought of my goodbye with Lisa out of my mind and I headed for the shower. I couldn't get over the Omni Hotel where we were staying. It actually had a telephone installed in the bathroom. Imagine!

The Terrace restaurant was almost full when Mom and I got there for breakfast, but the waiter guided us to a small table for two where we could gaze out on a garden and fountain. My mother was beaming with excitement. I hadn't seen her so happy since before my father had been killed. I looked out at the garden and remembered that terrible night the police officers had arrived to tell us about the accident on the freeway. It had occurred over two years before, and yet, sometimes it seemed so recent.

After that, my mother had stopped going out. She wouldn't go to the football games at the high school. She'd given up her drama courses at the college. Except for her work at the doctor's office, she had just stopped living. Now, here she was sitting across from me absolutely glowing. It seemed like old times. This trip would be so good for Mom. I wondered what it would be like for me.

I glanced up as a movement outside the window caught my attention. A woman was pulling at a hibiscus bloom. She must be an Easterner, I thought. Someone used to those flowers wouldn't bother to pick one. The woman stepped back, the yellow blossom in her hand. She put it to her nose, expecting an exotic smell, but I knew she'd be disappointed.

She handed the flower to someone who had just joined her beside the bush, a guy about my age or, maybe, a little older. He took his turn smelling the odorless blossom, and I laughed to myself. The boy was dressed in white jeans and a blue sport shirt. His hair was dark blond, but the morning sun brought out a few red highlights. He was about six feet tall, with hazel eyes, and he was very good-looking, I thought.

"You're poking at your eggs," my mother scolded. "Let's hurry so that we can see some of Miami before it's time to board the ship."

I dutifully began to eat, but for some reason I couldn't take my eyes away from the boy out in the garden. He was looking at a folder that the woman, probably his mother, had pulled out of her straw bag. They were evidently on a trip of some kind, and they pointed excitedly to some of the pictures in the brochure.

"He's quite nice-looking, isn't he?" my mother said, grinning at me.

"Who?" I asked, pretending to be terribly interested in my plate.

"Oh, you know who I mean," she said playfully.

Just then, the guy looked right at me. I knew he couldn't see me because the window was tinted, so I screwed up my face and gave him a totally awful look. *Take that, you handsome creature!* I said to myself. And for the next few minutes, while my mother paid the waiter, I sat and daydreamed about the boy. I imagined we were touring Miami by moped, sailing on a luxurious yacht, swimming in the coral-edged ocean.

My mother poked me in the ribs. "Kari, if we want to visit all of those wonderful shops and see the sights around here, we're really going to have to move it."

I shook myself out of my fantasy world and stood up. But before I left, I turned once more to take a peek at Prince Andrew. That's what I had started to call him in my mind. He and his mother looked so elegant, almost royal.

"Goodbye, Prince Andrew. Too bad I'll never see you again," I whispered, leaning into the basket of flowers that stood on the table.

"What?" my mother asked.

15

"Oh, nothing," I said. "I just wanted to smell the flowers."

"Did they have a nice scent?" she asked.

"They were silk, not real at all," I told her. *Just like my Prince Andrew*, I thought. *He isn't real. Not for me, at least.*

Chapter Three

Our taxi slid to a stop near the huge ship, which would be our home for seven days and nights. Dozens of other taxis were dropping off excited travelers, who dragged, tugged, and lugged all sizes and shapes of travel gear.

"I can't believe the size of this ship," I exclaimed to my mother, trying to catch my breath.

At least we didn't have to struggle with our suitcases. They'd been picked up earlier, one of the ship's extra services, and had been magically whisked off while we were shopping. We would find them in our cabin. We found a place in one of the many boarding lines. I turned and smiled broadly at my mother. Our adventure had begun! It took us half an hour to reach the registration window,

17

but it was kind of fun waiting because everyone around us was in such a good mood.

Finally we got to the front of the line, and my mother handed the man behind the little window our boarding passes and tickets. We were directed down a long hall toward the entrance to the ship. As we stepped aboard, a camera flashed in our faces. I was sure we were both smiling because we were so happy and excited about the trip. At last we were on board the S.S. *Norway!*

"I understand there will be a lot of picture taking," my mother said as we walked toward our assigned deck. "Then at the end of the trip, they post the photos, and we can purchase copies of whichever ones we want." She turned to a woman in a ship's uniform, who seemed to be waiting just to show us to our cabin. "Viking Deck, cabin V-O-fifty-six," my mother said. The woman gave us clear instructions, and soon we were walking down the hall that would lead us to our cabin.

We had to walk carefully because luggage was stacked all over the hall. And there on our left was our cabin with our familiar suitcases piled up against the wall.

Pushing the door open, I was happy to find the room as cozy and comfortable as I'd imagined it. It was painted a soothing blue with aqua-colored bedspreads on the twin beds. A charming little dresser was anchored to the floor, and there were two portholes high up on one wall. A small painting of an ocean scene hung above the dresser. We had a private bathroom with a nice shower and mirrored medicine cabinet.

"What are those funny handles for?" I asked my mother, pointing to two chrome bars by the toilet.

"In case of choppy seas," Mom explained. I tried to dismiss the words "choppy seas" from my mind. That I didn't need. "One thing to remember," she went on, "is to step over the thresholds of the ship. See?" She looked down at the floor in front of the bathroom. "You'll find a bar like this one in almost every doorway. Uncle Craig told me they're for water control and virtually every vessel in the world is built with them. But I know we'll both forget and stumble around for a few days."

There came a gentle tapping at the door, and I opened it to find a handsome, dark-skinned man in a white uniform smiling in on us. "I'm George," he explained in a lilting accent. "I am your cabin steward." We found out later that George was from Jamaica. He was very warm to us, and though I realized he had to go through his little speech in each cabin assigned to him, he treated us as though we were the only guests on the ship.

"As a safety precaution, we have a lifeboat drill before weighing anchor," he said. Then, catching my worried look, he added, "Actually, it's a lot of fun. It's good way to see the ship and meet some of your neighbors. Full instructions are on the back of your cabin door. I'll be back in about an hour to answer any questions you may have." He gave us a friendly salute and disappeared down the hall.

George was right about the lifeboat drill being nothing to worry about. The whole thing only took fifteen minutes, and we were back in our cabins once more. I wouldn't say it was fun, exactly, but it wasn't scary.

My mother looked down at her watch. "Come on, Kari, we just have enough time to unpack before we sail out of Miami. I want to be on one of the upper decks so we can see and hear the whole celebration."

I didn't realize how big that celebration was going to be until we climbed the stairs again and reached the ship's decks. A beautiful buffet had been set up at the outdoor restaurant on the International Deck. Streamers and decorations flew everywhere, dancing gaily in the breeze. Promptly at five the band struck up a lively song, and the ship began to move. We were sailing at last!

It was terrific to see the Miami skyline slowly slip away from us. Everyone waved madly when the blasts from the ship's horn ripped through the air.

"Oh, darn. I wanted to take some pictures," my mother yelled to me. "But I left the camera in our cabin!"

"I'll run down and get it," I shouted.

"Hurry," she said. "I'd hate to miss getting a picture of Miami in the setting sun. What a beautiful sight!"

I ran past Mom, stopping for a second to try to get my bearings. Once I found the stairs, I ran two flights down as fast as I could to the Viking Deck. What was it that one of the crewmen had said over the loudspeaker about the carpeting? To make it easier for the passengers to find their ways around, every deck was divided into two color-zones. The forward section had turquoise carpeting, and the aft zone had salmon pink. Or was it the other way around?

I stood still for a moment. I knew I was on

the right deck, but was I going in the right direction? The brochure had said the ship was three football fields long. How would I ever find my cabin?

I looked down at the carpet again. Definitely a salmon pink, but that didn't help me much now. Well, I decided, if I kept running around and around the ship eventually I would have to reach cabin V056. But by that time the sun would have set, Miami would be just a memory, and my mother would probably be wondering if I'd fallen overboard. Desperately I looked around for help. The brochure claimed that the ship had 785 crew members on board, all hired just to make our cruise as pleasurable as possible. But I couldn't even find one. The corridors were completely empty. Of course. Everyone else was on the upper decks waving goodbye to Miami.

Feeling like a mouse in a maze, I started down the corridor. As I thought about missing the celebration, I got more and more anxious and walked faster and faster, until I was actually running down the halls. I took this turn, then that, checking the cabin numbers on the doors and getting completely lost. I should have taken the time to study the floor diagram a little more closely. Finally, I was running on turquoise carpet, but I didn't know if that meant I was any nearer to my room.

Then I turned a corner and—*crash!* I slammed right into someone coming from the opposite direction. I blinked hard and reached for the railing on the wall as I lost my balance and began to fall. The person I'd crashed into grabbed me, and we landed in a crumbled heap together on the turquoise carpet.

I groaned, rubbing a sore spot on my forehead. Then I felt myself being helped to my feet. When I looked up, I got a shock. I was gazing into the stunningly handsome hazel eyes of my Prince Andrew! "Are you OK?" He sounded so concerned. Funny, I'd never heard his voice before, but it sounded exactly as I'd imagined it.

"I'm fine, I think," I told him, gingerly feeling my forehead again.

"Do you have a lump on your head?" he asked, brushing a strand of my hair out of my eyes.

"Not yet," I said, "but I may tonight." Just then two men and a woman came walking down the hall. Prince Andrew dropped his hands from my shoulders and stepped back so

23

they could get by. The group smiled as they passed us, as if to say, "Oh, look, young love."

The group disappeared around a corner, and Prince Andrew and I were alone again. For a moment neither of us said a word. "I'm trying to find my room," I said, just to fill the silence. I stood there, feeling awkward and hoping my blush would fade. I looked down at my watch. "I've got to find my cabin. Miami is disappearing fast, and Mom wants her camera."

With a charming smile, Prince Andrew asked, "What's your cabin number?"

"V-0-fifty-six. It sounds like some kind of hair spray," I added, giggling. "I know I'm on the right deck, but I can't locate the number!"

"You must have passed it," he said, looking at the number on one of the doors. "Let's see, it should be right down this next hall." He was right. There on the left was V056. "Do you want me to wait for you?" he asked. "I'm heading back to the deck anyhow."

"Oh, no," I told him. "I have a couple of things to do before I go back. Thank you, but I can make it on my own now." I don't know why I turned down his offer. There was nothing I would have liked better than to take a stroll along the deck with this handsome, poised boy. I hated to think that he'd probably already pegged me as a superklutz.

He stood there in the doorway, looking better and better every second. Then the worst thing happened. "Haven't I seen you before?" he asked curiously. "You aren't from Lancaster, Pennsylvania, are you?"

I sucked in my breath. "No, I'm from the West Coast, California. I've never even been to Pennsylvania."

"Oh." He stepped back now, ready to leave at last. I wondered if I'd meet up with him again later in the cruise. "I could have sworn I recognized you."

"Well, I don't remember seeing you before," I lied. Was it possible he'd seen me during breakfast?

"I guess I must be wrong. See you later." He smiled broadly. He turned to go, and I closed the door quickly with a mixture of relief and sadness. I knew I had a huge crush on that boy, but for some reason, I felt a little uncomfortable around him.

Now, where was that camera? I found it quickly, then checked my face in the bathroom mirror. My hair was a complete disaster! Fine, long blond hair gets ruined with even a little breeze. Hurriedly, I grabbed my brush and tried to smooth down my hair. It really wouldn't matter anyhow, it would be all over my face once I was back on the deck. But I hated to think of Prince Philip seeing me in that state. I locked the cabin door behind me and started for the stairs. Oh, no, where were they, anyway? I couldn't believe it, but I was lost again!

I peered down the hallway, trying to figure out where I was. And there, with his back to me, was Prince Andrew, walking at a fast pace. I stared at his retreating figure and held my breath. I didn't want him to know I couldn't find my way again. But then, he was my only guide back to the deck, so I followed quietly behind him, keeping a good distance away.

But when he came to a turn in the corridor, he caught a glimpse of me. He smiled and turned to face me. "You're not lost again, are you?" He grinned at me, his eyes laughing.

"Oh, no, I know my way perfectly."

"Well, we might as well go together," he said, and I could tell from the way he said it that he knew I didn't know where I was. But he was too polite to say as much.

"Might as well," I said, trying to sound casual.

We walked together to the International Deck. I could hear the band still playing. Eighteen hundred and fifty-four passengers shouted goodbye to the crowd on land. As the prince and I walked toward the outdoor restaurant, he gave my arm an excited squeeze. "This trip is already something special. I've got to find my parents and my sister," he said. "We promised to meet up here for that fantastic banquet they've set up."

I spotted my mother at the rail. She was waving frantically to some of the people in the crowd. It didn't seem to matter that she didn't know them. Anyway, it looked as though she'd forgotten completely about the camera and me.

"I see my family over there," the prince told me. We started to part when he caught my arm. "Oh, now I remember where I saw you before," he said. "It was the Omni Hotel, where we were staying. You were sitting in the restaurant, and I was in the garden with my mother. You gave me the funniest look!"

The ship lurched suddenly to one side, and I almost lost my balance. "But the windows were tinted—"

"Not *that* tinted." He smiled down at me.

"Oh-h-h," I groaned in utter embarrassment. "I wasn't making a face at you, I—um, my juice went down the wrong way."

He nodded his head thoughtfully as if he accepted my dumb story. Then, he put out his hand. "I'm Noah Walters from Lancaster, Pennsylvania."

"I'm Kari Langtree from Huntington Beach, California," I said, clasping his hand in a friendly, warm shake.

"Bon voyage, Kari," he said.

"And bon voyage to you, Prin—I mean, Noah," I said, allowing my hand to rest in his for a moment.

Then he disappeared into the crowd.

Chapter Four

"Do you have an early or a late seating?" George, the cabin steward, asked my mother.

"Late," she answered, watching him stack our empty luggage neatly in a corner. "We're assigned to the Windward Dining Room, table forty-four."

"A very good one," George said. "It's right beside the captain's table."

"Do we get to see him every night?" I asked.

"No, he has to divide his time between the two dining rooms, and the early and late seatings, so you might see him twice, maybe three times, according to his schedule. By the way, the late seating begins at eight-thirty."

I wondered if Prince Andrew—no, I would have to learn to call him by his real name—I wondered if Noah would be in our dining room. Probably, since his cabin was near ours. Now the question was, did he have an early or late seating? I would have to check around casually.

By eight-fifteen I had showered once, brushed my hair five times, and changed my outfit twice. I'd finally settled on a white cotton dress with a wide red belt and red leather sandals. I finished it off with my favorite red hair comb, which looked good against my blond hair.

"You look great!" my mother said, coming out of the bathroom.

I had to admit she looked fantastic, too. Her skin glowed with an inner excitement I hadn't seen for years.

We arrived at the Windward at exactly eight-thirty. The tables were all set romantically with flowers and tall candles. Table 44 was set for eight, and four of the other diners were already seated around it. Mom and I took our places and smiled at the others. A couple arrived, filling the table. We took a good look at one another, knowing that we would be sharing this table at every meal except, of course, when we chose to eat at the outdoor restaurant or the midnight buffet.

We introduced ourselves, and everyone

seemed pretty nice. There were three giggling girls, college students on a winter break vacation. The couple were honeymooners. They spent most of their time smiling at each other. The other diner was a loner. Ron Benjamin explained that he was a professional photographer, planning to take a lot of photos of Saint Thomas and Nassau, which he would sell to travel agencies. He seemed to be about my mother's age.

I stretched my neck to see if I could find Noah, but he was nowhere in sight. The elegant dinner began, and I busied myself with the delicious food, as did everyone at our table. The captain's table remained empty, although it was set for a banquet. Waiters brushed by with busboys rushing to keep up with them. The wine stewards poured glasses with great flourishes. Everyone agreed the meal was very special.

During dessert I watched as a birthday cake was brought out to a table in the corner of the room. The waiters grouped together and began their singing. ". . . happy birthday, dear Noah-h-h; happy birthday to you." I dropped my dessert spoon on the floor, and it was immediately replaced by a waiter. I smiled happily to myself and dug into my hot fudge

31

sundae. What luck! Unless Noah ran off to the outdoor restaurant for every meal, I could count on seeing him three times a day.

I watched him blow out the candles on his cake. He sat next to his mother, the woman I'd seen at the hotel. Across from him were his father and a beautiful girl. I figured she was his sister. Her hair was the color of honey and swirled around her shoulders like an expensive silk scarf. She looked about my age.

A few more birthday announcements were sung. It was happy birthday, dear Natalie, dear Jack, dear Marian, and finally, dear Gloria. After that they started on the happy anniversary songs, and our tablemates began to drift off to go to the evening entertainments. I sat watching the other diners for a while. My mother and Ron Benjamin were very involved in conversation. They decided to meet in the game room the next day for some backgammon. It had been Mom's favorite game, but she hadn't played since my father's death. Mom and Ron said their goodbyes, and we began to leave the dining room. I looked back for a moment at Noah's table, but the corner was empty.

Back in our cabin my mother moaned. "I

simply must go to bed. I'm exhausted, and it's been such a long day."

"Oh-h-h," I protested, "do we have to? I'm not a bit sleepy."

"Oh, to be so young!" She began to undress. "This is your vacation, too, Kari. Of course you don't have to go to bed when I do. There are all kinds of things happening on this ship. The schedule of events is on top of the dresser."

I walked over to the dresser and read the day's schedule. In the Windjammer Lounge there was folk guitar music. That was perfect for the bittersweet mood I was in. Without reading on, I decided I would go check it out. I loved to listen to guitar music, and maybe I'd meet some other lonely people. I strolled up to the International Deck. The Windjammer was just one of a dozen places where entertainment was held, so I figured no lounge would be too crowded.

But my hopes of drifting unnoticed to an empty table were soon smashed. The Windjammer was packed. I took a quick look around the darkened room to see if I could find a place, but it was no use. All the tables were crowded, and people even lined the back of the room. I saw a few empty seats, but I just didn't have the nerve to ask any of the groups if I could join them. The guitarist was on a break, anyway. I thought maybe I'd check the other lounges.

"Kari, over here!" a familiar voice called. Noah! "Over here," he called from a corner of the lounge. There he was at a small table, his beautiful sister at his side. I walked over, and he offered me a seat opposite him. "Kari, this is my sister Natalie."

"Hi, Kari," Natalie said warmly.

"Hey, Noah," I said, "I heard a birthday song. Congratulations."

"Don't forget to congratulate Natalie, too," he said.

"It's your birthday, also? Oh, now I remember. I heard your name right after Noah's."

"We're twins." Natalie laughed. "I know we don't look alike, but it's true."

"So we're sharing our seventeenth birthday," Noah explained.

A waiter came over and asked us if we wanted anything to drink. We ordered orange juices all around. The guitarist came on stage and began to play. We sipped our drinks as she sang some traditional folk song. Lisa loved this kind of music. It would have been so much fun to have her there, I thought, I wondered what she was doing and if she were thinking of me, too. I wondered if she missed me as much as I missed her.

"Have you ever seen so many Christmas trees in your life?" Natalie asked, bringing me out of my thoughts. "How many do you think there are on this ship?"

"Hundreds," I said. "They're all over this deck."

"And each one is decorated differently," Natalie went on.

"Nat, this woman is a great guitarist," Noah broke in enthusiastically.

Natalie's blue eyes crinkled as she smiled. "Kari, do you know that Noah plays even better than that woman up there?"

"My sister is a great fan of mine," Noah put in quickly, his face turning bright red. "And you should know that Nat sings beautifully. She's really the star in our family. But we sound pretty good together."

"Oh, Noah, don't brag," Natalie said.

"We're thinking of entering the ship's talent show," Noah said.

"I can't imagine getting up there in front of an audience," I told them. "I guess you have to have a lot of nerve."

"Actually, we don't usually play for others. My favorite thing to do is get together with some friends and sing," Natalie said.

"Hey, why don't we do that tomorrow, the three of us together," Noah suggested.

"When?" I asked.

"After breakfast. That is, if you don't have anything else planned."

"Oh, Noah, what a great idea." Natalie smiled. "Kari, you've just got to say yes."

"Boy, am I in demand here. And with such persistent invitations, how can I refuse?"

"Great!" Noah said.

"Excuse me, can I join you?" a voice broke into our conversation. The speaker was a boy, about eighteen. His hair was very dark, his smile friendly.

"Sure," Noah told the stranger.

"My name is Lasse Varberg, and I haven't made any American friends yet. You sound like you're having a good time."

Natalie introduced us all. "Where are you from? Norway?" she asked.

"A good guess," he said, laughing. "But I'm from Sweden." He sank into our extra chair and placed his soda on the table.

It took Noah and Natalie only a few minutes to make Lasse feel like he was one of

36

our group. Natalie soon had him talking about how he and his family came to be on the S.S. *Norway.* "I am a student at the University of Uppsala, and this trip is a Christmas present from my parents for all of us," he confided to us. He had a pleasant, crooked smile, and he laughed easily with us.

Noah told us that his family hadn't been anywhere together for two years. When he'd read about the S.S. *Norway* in the newspaper, he and Natalie had nagged their parents to go on the trip until they'd finally given in. I told them about Aunt Camille and Uncle Craig's present, and they all agreed that it was a terrific gift.

There was just one uncomfortable moment when Lasse asked me if my father hadn't wanted to go, too, and I quickly explained that he wasn't alive. But I was used to answering questions like that.

Pretty soon Lasse asked Natalie if she would like to walk with him on the upper deck, and she accepted quickly. I got the feeling those two had taken an instant liking to each other. After another round of orange juice, Noah and I decided to take a stroll, too. We stood up to go, and four people grabbed our table before we reached the door. Noah laughed. "Popular place."

I grinned up at him. "That must be because it's such a good spot to make friends."

Outside, the night air was cool and fresh. Noah and I stood alone on the moonlit deck. The moon paved a path of light across the dark water. "My whole family is staying in one cabin," he told me, looking into the night. "We used to go camping together in one big tent. That was years ago. We had the best times, all banging into each other. There was a lot of crabbing and complaining, but a lot of laughing, too. Somehow, I thought it would be the same when we talked about taking this trip. But it doesn't seem to be working out that way," he said sadly.

Talking so seriously with Noah made me realize how much I was beginning to like him. I didn't know what he was talking about exactly, but my heart went out to him, and I tried to say something that would cheer him up a little. "Noah, tomorrow might be a little sunnier."

Noah laughed, shaking off his sorrow. "Actually, I hear we're in for a bad storm. Just look at those dark clouds. So get ready for a little motion sickness, if you get that kind of thing."

"You mean, this huge ship will be rocking like crazy?"

"You bet. The ship has stabilizers, so we'll make out much better than the passengers on smaller ships. But there's a certain amount of rocking that you have to put up with."

"You sound like you've been on a ship before," I said.

"This is my first time on a big ship," Noah answered. "But I've gone for two-week fishing trips on commercial boats with my uncle. Still, that's different, too. You expect a lot of motion, and you get it!"

"The ocean seems to go on forever." I stared into the water. "It almost feels as if there's no land anywhere. As far as we can see, there's nothing but water. It's such a new experience for me. The only boat trips I've been on have been short sails to Catalina, where an aunt and uncle of mine live."

"What's it like in California?" Noah asked. "I've never been there."

"Well, in the winter when we want to play in the snow, we drive up to Big Bear. But on the same day, we can go to the beach and swim. People from the East say they miss the seasons, but I've never known seasons, so there's nothing for me to miss."

"How funny," Noah said. "I don't know if I'd like that."

We stood still for a moment, watching the moon scoot in and out of the storm clouds. Then, impulsively, Noah said, "I'm glad you're going to come and sing with us tomorrow. I like being with you."

"Thank you for inviting me," I replied.

"Do you like to sing?"

"Oh, I really enjoy it, but don't expect a wonderful voice. I've disappointed people with it before."

"What do you mean?" Noah asked.

"Well, my music teacher heard me singing to myself one day, and he asked me to try out for the school chorus. But when I got to the audition and had to get up there in front of the judges, I was so nervous, all that came out was a little squeak." We both laughed, and Noah moved closer to me. He put his arm around me, and we just stood there, enjoying being near each other.

It was strange, wonderfully strange, to be with Noah. He made me laugh about things that had driven me to tears not too long ago. Slowly I slipped into a daydream. Noah and I were driving up the California coast. Suddenly, when we turned a bend, there was the most perfect beach in the world. With only one glance, we both knew we had to stop and take a swim. We jumped out of the car and raced toward the cool water. . . .

Then it hit me. Noah wasn't going to be in California. We'd have seven short days together, by now only six, and then he'd go back to Pennsylvania. I'd let myself care for him, and once more, I'd be abandoned. Well, I wasn't going to let it happen again, not right after Lisa had left. "I've got to get back to my cabin," I said abruptly. "I'm really exhausted."

"OK, I'll walk back with you," Noah offered.

I peeked at him from the corner of my eye. A few more minutes with him wouldn't hurt, right? I could start staying away from him the next day. We ran down the stairs together, trying not to make any noise since it was already late. But the more we tried to be quiet, the more we began to giggle. By the time we got to the Viking Deck, we were laughing like two little kids. I really was amazed at the way Noah could get me laughing in spite of my worst fears.

At my cabin door Noah turned and said, "If you want to do some jogging with me tomorrow, I'll be running on the Oslo Deck before breakfast."

"Well, um, maybe," I said, hedging. Jogging on a ship's deck did sound awfully nice. But, no, I didn't want to get hurt again. I had to protect myself. I wasn't going running with Noah, and that was that.

"I'll be there," he said. "If you feel like it, just show up, OK?"

"Sure," I said. I opened my door, and Noah walked down the hall.

I undressed slowly, trying not to wake my mother. I pulled my robe on over my pajamas, and got out my sketch pad. I pictured Noah's face and began to draw. His dark blond hair was easy, and I drew a few strands falling over his forehead, as if a breeze were blowing. His smile was harder, but gradually his face took form.

I held the pad out to view my work. There was Noah, grinning happily at me. Suddenly my heart felt heavy, and I closed the pad with a snap. I was beginning to realize just how much I cared for him. And how hard it was going to be to stay away from him!

Chapter Five

"Boy, am I out of shape," I gasped as I jogged in the morning sun. I'd woken up thinking about poor Noah running all alone on the Oslo Deck. It didn't seem right to leave him there, especially after he'd been so friendly to me. Besides, I thought, the exercise would do me good. I convinced myself I wasn't cheating on my resolve not to see Noah because I'd have to meet him later to sing anyway. After all, I'd promised Natalie I'd be there.

Deep down, I knew these were all just excuses to be with Noah. *Watch out, Kari,* I warned myself. *You are setting yourself up for a lot of pain when this cruise is over and you never see that boy again.* But I knew I couldn't lie in bed when Noah was out there looking for me. No way!

"For someone who hasn't been running in

a long time, you're doing pretty well." Noah smiled at me.

"I used to jog all the time with my father," I said sadly. "I guess once I couldn't do it with him any more, it stopped being fun."

"But you're having fun now, aren't you?"

"I sure am," I admitted. Running usually brought me unhappy thoughts of my father. But I was really enjoying it now. Noah certainly had a talent for making me laugh at the things I was most afraid of. He'd done it the other night when I'd told him about the terrible chorus audition, and he was doing it again now.

"Wow, I didn't think so many people on this ship would be into running!" Noah exclaimed as the deck began to fill with early joggers.

"How's your family getting along in your one little cabin?" I asked.

"We're managing," Noah said. "I feel sorry for the people on either side of us, though, when my dad starts his search for his socks this morning. It's going to be awful. Mom told Natalie that she forgot to pack them."

"Your poor father! But it won't be long before your parents will kiss and make up," I told him. Noah didn't say anything and we jogged in silence for a few moments.

"They used to do that, kiss and make up," he said finally, "but they don't do it much anymore. Everything's a big deal now. It's funny. I looked forward to this cruise for three whole months. And now, I wish I hadn't ever heard of the S.S. *Norway*."

It was the same sadness he'd expressed the night before. I caught his arm and pulled him into a deck chair nearby. "Too tired to run and talk at the same time," I explained. "Now tell me why you don't like the *Norway*."

"Oh, it isn't the ship," he said, avoiding my gaze. "It's my parents. But, Kari, forget I said anything. None of this is your worry. Come on, we've got to get showered and dressed. It's almost time for our breakfast seating."

In the Windward Dining Room, I spotted Noah as he made his way to his assigned table. He raised his hand in a wave, and my mother watched me wave back. "Who's that?" she asked, putting down her menu as I settled myself in the seat. "Seems like I've seen him before."

"Remember the boy and his mother in the garden at the Omni Hotel?"

"Oh, yes," she said and smiled. "You mean they're on this ship, too? What a coincidence!"

"He has a twin sister, too," I added. "He plays the guitar, and she sings. We're all going to sing together after breakfast."

"That sounds lovely, Kari. You know, for a while there I was worried that you wouldn't have enough to do, but you're making friends already."

Breakfast was as perfect as dinner had been. I had apple pancakes with apple syrup and daydreamed the whole meal away thinking about Noah. Mom was engrossed in a conversation with Ron Benjamin, and the college girls hadn't come down for the meal, so there wasn't really anyone for me to talk to anyway.

Mom told me she and Ron were starting their backgammon match that morning, so after breakfast they said goodbye to me and went to the game room. Watching them walk toward the elevator together gave me a queasy feeling in my stomach, and I wasn't quite sure why.

As I went down the stairs to the Walterses' cabin, I hoped Noah would be less upset by now. At this point his father would have found out about the socks, and if Noah's parents were anything like mine had been together, their little misunderstanding would be over. I wanted to have a really good time with Noah now because I intended to avoid him after this. I was not going to risk a broken heart.

I found the Walterses' room and knocked gently. Natalie opened the door. "Glad you could make it," she said, smiling.

Noah, seated on one of the beds, his guitar already in hand, gave me a friendly wave. "Mom and Dad are out meeting some people at the pool, so we've got the place to ourselves," he said.

I found a comfortable chair and sat down. "Well, what should we sing?" I asked.

"Anything you want," Noah said, "as long as I can figure out the chords."

"Oh, you choose. You two are the musicians, I'm not."

"Why don't we start out with some old Beatles tunes," Natalie suggested. "They're always fun."

Noah found a guitar pick and began the introduction to "Yesterday." He played so tenderly and expressively. And Nat's voice was simply beautiful. The song came alive as the

47

two of them sang and played, and it was easy for me to join in. Usually I'm too shy to sing in front of others, like at the chorus audition. But with them, I didn't feel self-conscious, and I sang without thinking about it.

"I can't sing too long today," Nat told Noah after a few tunes. "My throat gets scratchy whenever I'm around the ocean."

"Then let's go swimming!" Noah suggested, propping up his guitar in a corner.

For a moment I thought of making excuses, but I was finding it pretty hard to turn down any of Noah's invitations. "I'll run back and get my suit," I said finally. We agreed to meet on the Pool Deck in fifteen minutes. Just as I was leaving, Mr. and Mrs. Walters came in.

"Oh," Mrs. Walters said, sounding a lot like Natalie, "you must be Kari. We've heard so much about you."

"If you're going swimming," Mr. Walters said, "you'd better hurry up. It's getting pretty windy out there, and a bit chilly. I hear we'll be hitting a bad storm soon."

As I walked down the hall toward my own cabin, the storm was the furthest thing from my mind. I'd found two wonderful friends. We all felt comfortable together and really enjoyed one another's company. But this was the last time I would spend with them, I told myself. I liked Noah too much, and I wasn't prepared to be hurt when the cruise was over.

I changed quickly into my favorite turquoise bathing suit and hurried to the pool. When I got there, I found that Lasse had joined Natalie and Noah. Mr. Walters had been right about the wind. It was vicious, but none of us really cared. We swam, played in the pool, talked, and snacked for our lunch. The afternoon was gone before we knew it, and we had to go to our cabins to get ready for a formal dinner.

"Let's hurry. I've got to look beautiful for the captain tonight," I said, laughing.

Noah leaned close to me and whispered softly in my ear. "If you went just the way you are now, you would be beautiful."

My heart melted and stiffened at the same time. *Uh-oh, Kari,* I thought. *You're already in over your head with this boy.*

My dress for the gala was all ready. It was the same gold one I'd worn to Lisa's wedding, but wihout all the fancy trimmings. I did my makeup the way I had seen Lisa do hers the day of the wedding. It seemed so long ago now.

I scrutinized myself in the mirror and then sat back, sighing out loud. I really did look good with my hair pulled back in a french braid. Noah thought I was beautiful. But I couldn't help being sad; I'd had my last day with him. And even meeting the captain couldn't make me feel better about that.

When Mom and I walked gracefully onto the International Deck a few minutes later, I spotted Noah's family already waiting in the long line to speak to the captain. They were far up front, so they didn't see us come in. I was glad of that. I didn't think I could handle talking to Noah right then. I was too sad about not being able to see him later.

He looked so handsome in his dark brown pants and tan jacket. All the swimming we had done that day had made his hair unruly, but I thought it made him look cute.

When Mom and I finally had our turns to talk to the captain, he was cordial and friendly. He made us feel as if we'd known him for years. After that we peeked into the Checkers Lounge, where a band was playing fifties songs. I saw Natalie, looking gorgeous as usual, dancing with Lasse, but I couldn't find Noah anywhere. Just as well, I thought.

I spotted Ron Benjamin in the crowd and

waved to him. He came over to us, smiling. "Judith, will you honor me with this dance?" He greeted me warmly and then turned all his attention to my mother. She took his arm, and the music swept them off. I stood alone, watching them.

He dances almost as well as my father used to, I thought. Suddenly I wanted to cry, and I dashed from the room for a breath of fresh, cool ocean air. I skipped the captain's dinner and went to bed early. I didn't want to watch Mom and Ron together.

Chapter Six

Monday morning a familiar ringing awakened me. I felt for the phone, but it wasn't there, someone had moved my bed stand. And then I remembered. I wasn't in my own bed back home, I was on the S.S. *Norway*, far out at sea. I got up sleepily. Whoever could be calling us? My mother turned over in her sleep as I picked up the receiver.

"Yes," I mumbled drowsily.

"Kari," Noah said, "I missed you at dinner last night."

"I wasn't feeling too well," I told him.

"Oh no, don't tell me you're seasick, too," he said. "Natalie can barely get up."

"Don't worry," I said. "I'm fine now."

"Great!" Noah exclaimed. "Then you can help me out. The steward slipped a notice under our door last night. The talent show is tonight."

"Yeah, so what's wrong, Noah? You're ready for it, aren't you?"

"No, you don't understand." Noah said. "Nat is absolutely wiped out. She can't sing."

"Oh, I'm sorry, Noah," I said, still half asleep. "But what's so awful about your going on alone? You're a wonderful guitarist."

"It won't be as good, Kari. The words mean so much in our songs. I definitely need a singer."

"Well, how can I help you?"

"Kari," Noah said, "I'm asking you to do Nat's part."

"You want me to do what?" I shrieked before I remembered my mother was asleep.

"Oh, come on, Kari, you know the words by heart."

"Of course I know the words," I told him, fully awake now. "But that doesn't mean I'm going to make a fool of myself—and you—by getting up there on that stage and singing!"

"It's a small stage."

"Oh, Noah, I'm sorry, but I can't."

There was a long pause on the other end, and Noah said goodbye. It was a nice, polite, calm goodbye. Mentally, I patted myself on the back. I'd finally stuck to my guns and turned down a chance to be with Noah. But deep down I knew if I weren't so darned afraid of an audience, I would have said yes to Noah in a second. As I sat thinking, I realized the ship was rocking terribly. No wonder poor Natalie felt so rotten.

"It sure is a rough ride today," my mother said, her voice weak and shaky.

"It feels a little like an earthquake, except the shaking keeps going on and on," I said. I stood up on the edge of my bed and parted the drapes covering the two sealed portholes. "Rain," I said, terribly disappointed. "And the waves are very choppy."

"We might as well get up," Mom said wearily. "I would have loved to sleep in, but I'm wide awake now, and I don't think I want to stay in bed with all of this rocking."

The phone rang again. I knew it was Noah. "You answer it this time," I said to my mother.

"I can't," she said, smiling. "I'm taking a hot shower."

I picked up the phone. "Yes?" I said impatiently.

"I'm coming to see you after breakfast,"

Noah stated. "With just a little practice, we can go on tonight."

Before I could say a word, the phone clicked in my ear. I crawled under the covers again and pulled them over my head. No way! I would not get up at the talent show and sing with Noah. I tried to visualize myself up on that stage. Noah and I were sitting on two high stools. He was playing beautifully, but as my terrible voice croaked out the words to the song, the crowd started to laugh. The laughter grew loud inside my head, and I moaned out loud. I could never go through that, not even for Noah Walters.

The heavy rain continued throughout breakfast. I forced myself to keep my eyes off Noah's table. The dining room was only half full, and one of the waiters said it was because so many passengers were seasick. The storm didn't bother me. Maybe I'd even take my sketch pad up to the International Deck and try to capture the swirling of the ocean. Just so I wouldn't run into Noah.

But after breakfast I decided not to risk going back to the cabin for the sketch pad after all because I knew Noah would be waiting for me there. I walked with my mother to the card room, where she was going to play backgammon with Ron. I sat with them for a while. Then I went into the gift shop. As I was poking around the cosmetics and perfumes, I was startled to hear a familiar voice behind me. "I thought I'd never find you. I was even considering having you paged."

I turned, and there Noah was, looking absolutely desperate. I looked at his sad face, and I knew I couldn't give him the brush-off, not then. "How's Nat feeling?" I asked.

"Still not too good," Noah said. "Hey, listen, it's stopped raining, so they're going to be serving lunch at the outdoor restaurant. If you want to go there instead of the dining room, we could eat together."

"I'll have to let my mother know," I told him. "I could go back to the cabin and leave her a message."

And so it was agreed. Noah went with me to my cabin where I wrote my mother a quick note. Then we went up to the deck and found two large chairs that were out of the wind. Later we ate hot dogs and salad, with ice cream for dessert. The sun shone bright and beautiful now, and the only reminders of the rain were a few wet spots on the deck that hadn't dried. The rocking had lessened, but it was definitely still there.

"You know I'm surprised at your lack of self-confidence," Noah said, taking a bite of ice cream.

"Who said I don't have any self-confidence?" I asked.

"You did," Noah said, "when you decided not to sing with me."

"That doesn't mean I have no self-confidence, it means I know I can't sing."

"But that's absolutely untrue. You have a very nice singing voice. I heard it myself, so you can't deny it."

"Listen, Noah," I said, starting to get angry. "I did tell you that the chorus was not too thrilled with my voice."

"Sure, I remember. You said you squeaked, but that was only because you were nervous."

"Of course I was nervous. And I'd be nervous again if I had to get up on a stage. I'd sound like a creaky door, and I'd totally ruin your song."

Noah didn't say anything for a moment. "Let's go back to my cabin and visit Nat," he said suddenly. "She'd love some company."

In the Walterses' cabin Natalie was propped up in bed. A wet cloth lay on her forehead, and she looked positively miserable.

"Hi, Kari," Mrs. Walters said. "I'm glad you two are here. I wanted to go to an exercise class, but I didn't want to leave poor Natalie alone." She grabbed a leotard, waved goodbye, and went out the door.

I sat down on the edge of Nat's bed, and she moaned. "Ooh, don't rock the bed any more than it already is."

"Oh, I'm sorry," I said, quickly moving over to one of the chairs. Noah picked up his guitar and started strumming it softly.

"Sing me something," Natalie said. "I've been lying here all morning with nothing to do."

"Come on, Kari, let's try to cheer her up," Noah said. He started playing and singing "Yesterday," and in a few moments, I joined him.

Noah had a fine voice, and in parts of the song he improvised a harmony, letting me carry the melody. We sounded really good, if I had to say so myself.

We went through it once, and Noah put down the guitar. "You have a sweet voice, Kari. And, you're right on key. Let's try it again." I looked over at Nat, and she nodded. Our music seemed to be making her feel less sick. We did the song again, and this time it was even better.

"You two sound great together!" Natalie exclaimed. "Your voices blend very well."

"Are you feeling up to a little walk on the deck?"

"I do feel a lot stronger," she admitted. She picked up her robe. "But don't stop playing now. Sing me another while I get dressed."

Noah and I sang the old Linda Ronstadt song, "Heart Like a Wheel," while Nat was dressing in the bathroom. "You know," Noah said when we finished, "I never sang with Nat. Her voice is so strong, I never thought she needed it."

"But I do?" I asked and laughed.

"Oh, I didn't mean it to come out that way," Noah said quickly.

"But it's true," I told him. "You didn't insult me. I know I have a weak voice. It's on key, like you said, but it's weak."

"It could be developed with the right breathing and practice," Noah said. "You have a soft, warm quality. I like it."

We ran through "Heart Like a Wheel" again, and by that time, Nat was ready to go. We walked slowly around the International

Deck. Noah looked down at his watch. "Oh, it's almost three."

"What's at three?" I asked.

"The deadline for the talent show. If I'm going to be in it tonight, I have to go to the Checkers Lounge and sign up. Anybody want to come with me?"

"I think," Natalie answered, "I'll just sit here for a while in the sun. Maybe Lasse will pass by."

Not wanting to stick around in case Lasse did show up, I decided to go with Noah. "I'll tag along," I said.

"We have to run back to my cabin first," he told me. "I've got to pick up my guitar."

"You mean you have to perform now?"

"Just a quick run-through so they can schedule everything," he explained.

We entered the lounge about ten minutes after three, and already there was a line. One man was softly playing a piano, and another was standing at the mike trying to adjust the wires. A third was testing the sound system. A girl about my age nervously dropped all of her sheet music. We got in line behind a man about sixty years old. He was telling another man that he would be singing an Irish song. They were joking and laughing together.

I didn't pay attention to Noah registering because my attention was taken by a man at the mike who was telling jokes to a ghost audience. He was laughing so hard at his own humor, he could hardly even finish one joke. After he registered, Noah pulled me aside, and we listened to the other performers as we waited for his name to be called.

Finally a man said, "Next up, Noah Walters—and Kari Longtree."

Noah tugged on my arm. "We're on."

"No!" I shook my head violently.

"Just sing the way you did in the cabin," he whispered to me. "If you can't do it once we get up there, it's OK. I'll just sing alone. Hey, I need you. I've never done this without Nat."

He dragged me to the stage and shoved me onto one of the stools. He plopped himself on another. "I'll start," he whispered to me. "Just sit with me to give me courage. You don't have to do a single thing if you don't feel like it. If you want to join me, come in anywhere in the song. It will sound as though we planned it that way."

Noah started to sing "Heart Like a Wheel." He looked at me as though I were the only one in the room, the only person who mattered. The people had quieted down and were lis-

61

tening intently to the beautiful sounds of Noah's guitar and voice. Somewhere in the third line I let my voice join his softly. He slipped into a harmony and nodded for me to carry the melody. Before I knew it, the song had come to an end, and the whole lounge was clapping enthusiastically.

"Hard act to follow!" one man shouted. I could hear other comments of encouragement, and they made me smile. Finally I was laughing happily out loud. Then, Noah reached over and grabbed my shoulders. He kissed me, full on my lips, in front of all those people! I'll never forget it.

"We can do it just as well tonight," he whispered to me. "The only difference will be a few more people in here."

Gently he helped me off the stool and put his arm around my waist. Suddenly I knew for certain that I couldn't stay away from Noah. It felt too wonderful to be with him. All I could do was brace myself for the time when I would lose him and get ready for a lot of pain.

Chapter Seven

That night as Noah and I sat in the café waiting for the talent show to start, I had second thoughts about the whole thing. What had I gotten myself into? Was I really going to sing in front of all those people, just because the boy I liked had asked me to? I knew love was dangerous, but this was too much.

Across the table from me, Noah looked as relaxed as could be. He smiled soothingly at me. "Don't be nervous, Kari. Everything is going to go beautifully. With you and me together, we can't miss."

"I would hate to dissappoint you, Noah," I said softly, "but if I freeze up, it will be just awful."

Noah smiled. "Kari," he said, reaching out and taking my hand gently, "what's the very worst thing that can happen?"

I thought a minute. "Oh, I guess they'll all laugh."

Noah broke into a grin. "Ha! Would that be so awful? Most of these people took this cruise to do just that, to laugh, have fun, and get away from the rest of the world. So we make them laugh. That's not bad at all." He gave my hand a tender squeeze. "You know what most of them will be thinking anyway? They'll be saying to themselves, 'Wow, I wish I had the guts to get on that stage and sing like that.' "

"You really think so?"

"Sure," Noah said.

"Oh, I don't know." Suddenly I felt depressed and scared again.

"Kari," Noah whispered, "no matter what happens up there, it's not the end of the world. We still have each other."

"Yes," I said softly, but I added to myself, *Only for a few more days.*

"Are you ready to go?" Noah asked.

"I'm ready." We got up together and walked silently to the lounge. We were on last, so we found two comfortable chairs and sat backstage listening to the show. Some of the performers were as good as any professionals, and others were terrible. But the audience clapped politely no matter how bad they were. I was thankful for that. I'd had this awful feeling that after we sang, they'd throw rotten tomatoes at us.

I knew my mother was out there with Ron. Noah took a quick stroll around the lounge and said that Natalie was there with Lasse and that his parents were sitting in the front row. They'd come early to get good seats. So just about everyone I knew on board would be listening. In addition, the show was being taped for the ship's closed circuit television, and most of the passengers would probably see it eventually. Wow, was that thought bad for my nerves.

Noah sat very close to me, his comforting arm around me. "As I told you during the run-through," he whispered, "just go up with me. Then, if you want to join the singing, great."

I swallowed hard. "OK."

"Don't worry, it will go fine no matter what."

Suddenly I heard our names called. My feet seemed to move on their own, and soon, I found myself on the stage in front of everyone. We slid onto two stools, and Noah adjusted the mike. A hush fell over the crowd. Noah put his guitar strap over his shoulder. For a moment, he just looked at me. "Smile, Kari," he whispered and began playing the introduction to "Yesterday."

Then, he began singing. Soon, I found myself coming in, and when he was sure that I would be comfortable with it, he switched to the harmony. Our voices meshed perfectly, and the people in the crowd seemed to hold their breaths.

I began to sing more surely. "Yesterday, love was such an easy game to play. Now I need a place to hide away . . ." It was true. A few days ago I hadn't even known Noah. Now, I was certain that I loved him but I was losing him, too.

I was so engrossed in the song, I barely realized we were coming to the end. The applause thundered through the lounge, and I forgot my sad thoughts. Someone called out, "Sing another." The crowd shouted agreement, and before I knew it, Noah was beginning "Heart Like a Wheel." This time I wasn't even scared. The song took over, and I sang as if my life depended on it. Afterward the audience cheered!

It was Noah who pulled me away from the whirl of compliments offered by family, friends, and strangers alike. We escaped to the enclosed portion of the International Deck to watch the late-night rain beat against the windows. A few times people waved at us, calling out that they had enjoyed our act. But after a little while, we had all the privacy we wanted.

We talked about the other performers and the night's excitement. Somehow, the subject of my father came up, and I found myself opening up to Noah in a way I had never been able to do with anyone else.

I pressed my face against the glass and felt the vibrations of the storm. "I wonder what it would be like to be out there in that rainy darkness, to be on the other side of this glass." We sat in silence for a moment. "Natalie and Lasse seem to like each other," I said after a while.

"Yes," Noah agreed. He seemed to be deep in thought, too.

"Your mother is really beautiful, Noah," I said. "Both your parents seem like very nice people."

"I don't think it's working," he said sadly.

"What's not working?" I asked, puzzled.

"My dad and mom together. And the reason for this whole trip," he answered, staring out into the black night.

I remembered he'd said his family hadn't been on a trip together for two years and that he and Natalie had talked their parents into the cruise. "Tell me about it," I said. "Maybe you'll feel a little better."

Noah sighed. "For at least a year, my parents have been going their separate ways. Mom's getting back into modeling, and Dad is busy researching a book he's writing. The more they throw themselves into their work, the bigger the rift between them becomes."

"So this trip was to try to close that rift."

"Something like that. Nat and I wanted it to be like old times again, like when we used to go camping and stuff."

"And what's not working?"

"Nat seems to think it is, but I don't agree."

"When will you know for sure?"

"Nat says to wait until the cruise is over. Still, listening to my parents argue today, I'd say the cruise is already over for them."

"But they looked so happy together at the talent show. You could be wrong. You don't know for sure yet."

Noah put his hand under my chin and

tilted back my head. "There's only one thing I know for sure," he said, "and it's that I want to kiss you." His lips met mine, and in that instant we both forgot all our troubles.

Chapter Eight

Our little travel alarm buzzed Mom and me awake early the next morning. We had a whole day in Saint Thomas, and we wanted as much time as possible on the island. "Mom," I said groggily, "Noah asked me if I'd spend the day with him. Would you mind very much if I went with him instead of you?"

Mom got out of bed and wrapped her robe around her. "Of course I wouldn't mind. Go and have a good time."

"Mom—" I hesitated.

"What is it, Kari?"

"I guess I'm just—just a little scared."

"Oh, honey, whatever for?"

"Well, I—I have so little time with Noah. Maybe it's not such a good idea to get involved with him. I mean, what's the point if I won't ever see him again after the cruise is over?"

70

My mother came over to me and sat down on my bed. "Who gave you such a silly idea?" she asked, smiling. "The point is, you seem to enjoy spending time with each other. Why, without Noah, you wouldn't have discovered your lovely singing voice and your charming stage presence. Good friends are hard to come by, so treasure Noah's company while you have it."

"But it hurts so much when someone leaves you. After Lisa left, I decided I never wanted that pain again."

"Kari," Mom said seriously, "when your father died, it hurt more than anything ever could. But I had twenty-three beautiful years with him. Do you think I should never have married him just because I was afraid I'd lose him one day?"

"Oh, Mom," I said, "I never thought of it that way."

My mother smiled. "Good, then that's settled. You'll go off with Noah, and you won't worry about next week, right?"

"Right," I agreed.

Mom brushed a few strands of my hair out of my eyes. "Can I ask you a question, Kari? Would you have minded if Ron had gone with

71

us today into Saint Thomas—if it had been the three of us?"

"No, of course not." I reached for my hairbrush. I saw Mom smile, and I knew my answer had made her happy. But I wondered how I would really have felt if Noah hadn't invited me and I'd found myself in that situation.

"It's too bad we won't have much time on the island. The last tender leaves Saint Thomas at three this afternoon."

The tender was the boat that transported people from the *Norway* to shore. Because the ship was so huge, it couldn't pull in too close to port, so, tucked away in the ship, were two eighty-foot tenders. Each one could carry four hundred passengers, and they were strong enough to take all the battering and thrashing of the waves close to shore.

I got dressed quickly, waved goodbye to Mom, and made my way to the Pool Deck. There was Noah, standing in line for a tender. "Hi, Kari," he said. "For a few minutes, I got worried that you'd changed your mind about going with me."

"Well, I was waiting to see if the captain would make an offer for my company. When he didn't call, I figured I might as well try to make your day a good one," I joked.

"Ha!" Noah said, pulling me over to him and giving me a quick kiss on the cheek.

In minutes we were off, leaving our huge floating hotel for the shores of Saint Thomas. Noah and I snuggled cozily on the upper deck of the tender. The sea had calmed, and the water had turned into a glasslike surface.

"Oh, I forgot!" Noah dug into his bag. "I grabbed two breakfast rolls from the outdoor restaurant. Have one."

"How can we get around the island?" I asked him in between bites. "I mean, you haven't signed up for one of the ship's tours, have you?"

"The tours are OK, but I know my way around Saint Thomas pretty well," he said. "I've been there twice with my father. He's had writing assignments here."

"What kind of writing does he do? You said last night he was researching a book."

"He's kind of well known on the East Coast. He writes a newspaper column about traveling."

"That sounds like fun."

"Kari," Noah said suddenly, "don't say anything to Nat about what I told you last

73

night. She's very sensitive about my parents' problems."

"I won't say a word," I promised.

Noah kept my hand in his as we stepped off the tender. There were hundreds of cabs, vans, and buses lined up to meet us.

"If you don't mind, let's walk," Noah said. "It's only a short distance to the shops and other places I want to show you. Then, later, we can take a moped ride up to Coral World. There are all kinds of interesting sites along the way."

"Sounds fine to me," I told him. I could have walked with Noah for miles and never gotten tired.

He took my hand, and we started up the hill. I smiled to myself. Mom had been right. The day was only just beginning, and I was having a wonderful time already, much better than if I'd been worrying about leaving Noah. I relaxed and enjoyed his closeness. The sky was brilliant and cloudless, and the treasures of Saint Thomas lay ahead of us.

We walked slowly, passing buildings that were a hundred years old and more. Noah told me all he knew about the many historical sites, and I read out loud to him from my guidebook.

On a narrow street, nestled between busy shops, we found an old church, built three hundred and fifty years ago. We passed the Hotel 1829, named for the year it was constructed. It was at the top of a long flight of steps cut directly into a hill. We stopped at an old synagogue with a floor made of sand.

"Hey, I'm exhausted already," I said, collapsing on a crumbling stone wall. Noah came over and sat down beside me. "Wouldn't this be a great way to study history?" I said. "Everyone would sign up if the course were taught this way. Instead of reading about the places, you'd go and touch and smell and see them."

"What a great idea," Noah said. "Even little things would become interesting that way. For instance, this stone wall we're sitting on has probably been here for centuries. Maybe pirates sat here, waiting for their ships to sail, watching the well-dressed Danish merchants rush by."

"I can almost see them now. Wow, just imagine, here we are, two Americans from a luxury cruise ship, sitting on the same wall another young couple sat on centuries ago. Maybe the girl was the daughter of a rich Danish merchant."

"And the guy was from one of the pirate ships docked in the harbor. They fell in love."

"And they wanted to marry, but the rich father wouldn't hear of it," I added to our story.

"So the pirate was planning to steal the girl away one night. His whole crew was in on it."

Noah and I lapsed into our own private dreams. I wondered about our imaginary couple. Had people like them ever really existed, and what had become of them? And what would happen to Noah and me in the years to come?

I stole a look at him. What was he thinking of? Was it this place and all its history, his parents and their problems, or possibly me? I wondered if, centuries from now, another girl and boy would sit on this same wall and imagine a couple from the 1980s just like Noah and me. We would be far in the past by then.

"What do you say we go for a ride on those mopeds?" Noah asked, interrupting my thoughts.

"Great!" I said. "I've never been on one, but I guess if I can ride a bike, I can manage a moped."

We stopped at the nearest stand and

76

rented two mopeds. I noticed a sign that said Drive On The Left At All Times. The man behind the counter smiled at me. "That sign is important. You have to remember to drive on the other side of the road, like in England. Also, there are almost no traffic lights on the island, so look out!"

And with those words of warning, we were off. It took me a couple of blocks to get used to the moped. And, boy, was it strange to ride on the left side of the road. Noah shouted to me that we were passing by Bluebeard's Castle. Over the put-put of the motors, he told me some of the legends of Bluebeard. "One story claims he had seven wives. One of the wives invited the other six to tea and poisoned them all. She was saved from the gallows at the last moment by her husband."

He pointed to a tower on a hill. "That's part of the castle, the tower named after Edward Teach. He was a pirate in the early eighteenth century, and that's where he stored all his loot."

"Wow," I said, "I bet he could store a lot of stuff up there."

The afternoon sun shone brightly as we rode up Skyline Drive. The road ran across a ridge of mountains, and the view was spectacular. With each slight turn in the road, we could see the sparkling blue Caribbean Sea. The town, Charlotte Amalie, lay cuddled in the valleys to the north. "It's too bad we can't stay longer," I said to Noah as we parked our mopeds near the white domes of Coral World. "I wish we could have the whole day in Saint Thomas."

We headed for the underwater observation tower. Inside, a staircase spiraled down fifteen feet under water. The walls were all glass, and we looked out into the open sea, where hundreds of tropical fish swam and played as though they had been waiting for us to arrive. Butterfly fish, trumpet fish, and parrot fish stood on their heads and did back flips and somersaults in between the blooming coral and slithering seaweed. I shuddered a little when, occasionally, a squid or octopus wiggled into the scene.

As we climbed the glass staircase, the scene changed dramatically. We saw sting rays, barracudas, sharks, giant eels, and lobsters. "It's a whole different world down there," I said to Noah. "I wonder what the fish think when they see our noses pressed against the glass."

"They probably think, 'It's a whole different world out there,' " he said. We walked slowly up the staircase, watching as the types of sea creatures changed at each new height. After that we went to explore the Marine Gardens, a twin-domed building with smaller sea scenes in saltwater tanks. Tiny sea horses held on to the stems of plants, looking like little windup toys. Eels darted in between slippery rocks. My favorite was a display of coral under ultraviolet light. The coral shimmered lavender and gold.

"What an incredible place," I said as Noah and I got back on our mopeds and headed toward town.

"I'm glad I was the one to show it to you," he said sincerely. Then we found a secluded bench by the edge of the sea and sat down to talk. We still had a little time before the tender left.

"You've done a lot of traveling, haven't you, Noah?" I asked.

"Yes," he answered, shaking a pebble out of his shoe, "and I love it."

"You're so lucky to have both your parents," I said wistfully. "And you have a great sister."

"But what about Lisa?" he asked.

"Well, she's not living at home anymore.

And my father is gone. I don't know, sometimes I feel like I'm losing my whole family."

"I've seen your mother with that guy who sits at your table. Is that bothering you?"

"No," I lied.

"Funny, I got the impression it did."

"Oh, I guess it bothers me a little. I mean it's strange to see my mom with someone else. I suppose I'm jealous. Do you think that's crazy?"

"No, I'm sure I'd feel the same way. In fact, if my parents break up, and I think they might, I know it will be hard to see either of them with someone else." Noah turned to me suddenly. "Do you have a boyfriend, I mean, someone you date all the time?"

I grinned at him. "No, I don't date anyone—yet."

He looked down at the cobblestones, a shy, embarrassed look on his face. "Would you write back if I sent you letters?"

"Sure," I answered. "In fact, I'd like that very much."

"I want to buy you something," Noah said, pulling me up. He seemed to know exactly where he was going. We ran down one of the passageways until we came to a musty-smelling store. He wouldn't let me see what he was buying until we were out in the sun. "I want it to sparkle for you," he explained.

On the street I opened the little white box. Inside was a gold chain with four golden letters hanging from it. L-O-V-E, they spelled.

"I wanted to buy you something that would last," Noah said, "not a flower or a souvenir. I wanted you to have something to help you remember me."

"Oh, Noah, how could I ever forget you," I said.

Later, as the tender pulled out of the harbor, I thought, *Maybe, someday, I'll come back. But it will never be the same, unless Noah is here with me.*

And then I remembered what Aunt Camille had said to me that night I'd told her I never wanted to fall in love. "When you do have to leave each other, you'll have many wonderful memories to keep you company." I glanced at Noah with Saint Thomas receding behind him. It would be a perfect memory.

Chapter Nine

We had barely stepped from the tender onto the S.S. *Norway* when the sky, so clear earlier, ripped open, sending down torrents of rain. The whole thing happened suddenly and with pounding force, not gently as it did at home.

A country fair celebration was scheduled for nine-thirty outside on the International Deck, so everyone was hoping the rain would stop. There were to be old-fashioned carnival booths and strolling clowns, musicians, hot dogs, and cotton candy. "If it clears up," Noah said as we walked toward my cabin, "let's just skip dinner and meet at the fair. I'll see if Nat and Lasse want to join us."

"Great," I said. "See you there. And, Noah, thanks for a beautiful day." I kissed him lightly on the cheek.

"With thanks like that, it is *definitely* my pleasure," he said teasingly.

I pushed open the cabin door. Mom was resting on her bed with her shoes off. She smiled at me. "Did you have a good time, Kari?"

"Terrific!" I told her. "Did you?"

"Beautiful," she said. "I think Ron and I went into every shop on the island. What's that around your neck?"

I bent down to show her. "Noah bought it for me."

"It's precious," she said, examining the golden letters. "I brought something back from the island, too." She reached over to the dresser and picked up a box. "Perfume. Ron bought it for me. It's called Forever. Have a smell."

A gentle lilac scent escaped from the delicate glass bottle. "I love it," I told her.

"We had a wonderful day," she said, resting back on the pillows again, "but it was exhausting. I got back just before you, and I thought I'd rest for a while before dinner."

"I think I'll try that, too," I said, pulling off my sweater and shoes and getting into bed.

The ship's rolling made my bed feel like a

baby's cradle, so cozy and inviting. It was easy to close my eyes and relax.

"Kari?" Mom asked. "Do you like Ron? I mean, what do you think of him?"

Taking time to choose my reply carefully, I answered, "He seems to be a nice man, but I don't know him too well. You keep taking over all the conversations with him," I said.

Mom laughed. "I guess I do. Kari, I like him very much. And he seems to like me. Although he came on this trip to do his photography work, he spends a lot of time with me. I was wondering how you felt about it. I suppose I should be with you more often."

"Oh, Mom! Of course he wants to spend all his time with you. You're the best-looking woman on this whole cruise! As well as the nicest, the most interesting, and the smartest."

She gave a lovely, tinkling laugh. "Kari, I think you're somewhat biased."

"But you *are* beautiful," I persisted.

Mom pushed her hair out of her eyes and sat up in bed. "Kari, I want to share some of my feelings with you. For a long, long time I didn't feel pretty or attractive at all. The last time I felt beautiful was the last time I kissed your father. I always felt beautiful with him.

He had a special way about him. Even when we went to parties, when both of us were talking to other people, he still knew exactly where I was, his eyes would find mine. Even when we were surrounded by many people, we had a special way of communicating."

"Mom," I whispered, "I always knew how it was between you two. And now, I think I'm really beginning to understand it for myself." At that moment I felt as if we weren't mother and daughter, but two very close friends who needed to tell each other the secrets of our hearts.

"Kari, it's happening again," she said. "I thought I could never fall in love after your father. But now, someone has made me feel beautiful once more."

Slowly I sat up in bed. "Mom, I'm glad for you." The words tumbled out of me, but a dull pain settled in my chest. Part of me really felt those words, but another part wanted to cry out just the opposite. Mom slipped quietly out of her bed and sat down next to me. She reached out her arms, and I slipped into her hug.

But even as we embraced, I wondered why I couldn't tell her how I really felt. Our lives were changing enough now with Lisa gone.

Why couldn't we go more slowly? She and I had always been the ones in the family who hated change; why was she doing this to us now? I closed my eyes and tried to see my perfect memory of Noah with Saint Thomas behind him. It was gone.

Like a miracle the rain stopped at about eight-thirty. When Nat, Lasse, Noah, and I met on the International Deck, all that was left of the storm was a little wind, and that didn't bother us. We spent a wonderful half hour throwing darts at tiny yellow, green, and red balloons, making spin-art paintings, and eating up pink cotton-candy cones. Then, the rain started up once more. I'd never seen weather change so quickly. The ship's crew decided to hold the barbecue, but, of course, it would have to be in one of the dining rooms. That took a lot of the fun out of it.

The four of us watched sadly through the closed glass doors as the rain slammed onto the sleek wooden deck. Deck chairs tipped over, and before the crew could grab and stack them safely, they blew in all directions. Lightning cut jagged openings through the sky. Huge waves slashed against the sides of the ship, and the boat rocked more than ever. We laughed a lot as we struggled to remain standing in the tossing ship, but I think we were all a little nervous, too.

Despite all that, the storm didn't lessen our appetites. We joined the hungry group in the dining room, piling our plates high with juicy ribs and chicken. "Listen, I have a great idea for the masquerade party on our last night," Lasse said excitedly as we found an empty table.

"Well, let's hear it," Natalie said.

"You see, I thought all four of us could go as something together."

Noah laughed. "What? Four blind mice?"

"Listen," Lasse said, looking around and pulling his chair in closer. In a secretive whisper, he presented his idea.

At first Natalie said no. "Why can't I go like the rest of you? Why do I have to be different?"

"Don't you want to win?" Lasse asked her.

"It's a brilliant idea, Nat," I said, trying to persuade her. "But where do you think we can find the stuff for her costume?"

"In the schedule of today's announcements," Lasse said, pulling a folded sheet out of his back pocket. "It says that the ship's crew will provide any materials they have."

"Then I'll help you make it," I told Natalie.

"Well—" She pursed her lips.

"Say you'll do it!" Lasse egged her on. "You'll be a beautiful mermaid, and the rest of us will be the fishermen who caught you." He smiled at her and reached out for her hand. "We'll win for sure. It'll be a piece of cake."

"That reminds me," Nat said, jumping up and not giving him an answer. "Where are those chocolate eclairs I saw?"

At least she wasn't getting seasick again.

After a little thought, Natalie agreed to the idea, and the next morning she and I met to work on her costume. I had invited her to my cabin because I knew we could be alone. Mom and Ron were playing backgammon and would be gone for hours.

As it turned out, we were lucky when it came to the materials for the costume. The crew had stacks of leftover Christmas decorations perfect for a glittering mermaid. Nat's idea was to wear her gold bikini, wrap a decorated sheet around her, and make some kind of crown to put over her long, blond hair. I knew I could count on my mother's travel and sewing kit for the needles, thread, and scissors. Nat spread the materials out on my bed, and I began to go through Mom's things trying to find the sewing kit.

"I brought money along in case we have to buy something in one of the stores," Natalie said. "But I hope we have everything we need right here."

"I think we'll manage. With a little imagination, we should be able to come up with something."

"But how do we make my crown? Maybe we could decorate some hair combs."

"I know just the thing," I told her. "The back of my sketch pad is thick cardboard. We'll cut it out in the shape of a crown and glue on some gold glitter. Look, there's a full jar here. Then we can sew this silver and gold trim onto the sheet the crew gave us. These sequins could even look like fish scales. Nat, this is going to be some costume!"

We started sorting through the shining materials and spent the next few hours sewing and gluing. Then someone knocked at the door. It was George.

"I wanted to show you something, Miss Longtree." He walked over to the television and turned it on. The tape of the talent show was being played, and there I was, walking onstage with Noah.

"You look great, Kari," Natalie said.

"I wish my mom could see this," I said.

"The tape will be run again tonight," George said. "I'll check with the office and find out what time. Now, hush, you're about to begin the first song."

George watched with us until the end of the act. He thanked me for letting him enjoy it with me, and then he disappeared down the hall.

Natalie and I collapsed in the middle of my bed. "Oh, Kari," she said, "you two really work well together, that was great. You were both so good."

"It was fun," I told her. "I was so scared for a while, though. Could you tell?"

"No way," she said. "You should have seen Noah and me when we were only seven and we performed in the spring festival at our school. We were so nervous we could barely stand up."

"Seven!" I exclaimed, laughing. "I wish I had been there. What did Noah look like way back then?"

"Wait a minute, I have a picture of us both when we were four. You'll love it." She slid off the bed and got her bag from the coffee table. "Once in a while I blackmail Noah by telling him if he doesn't do something for me, I'll

90

show this picture to his friends. He positively hates it." She found her wallet and pulled it out.

"I know how he feels," I told her, watching her flip through several photos in her wallet. "I hate the old one of me my mother carries."

Natalie handed a small picture to me. And there he was, a little Noah, as cute as could be. His hair was flying in all directions, and his arm was around his sister, beautiful even at the age of four. "How can he hate this? He's adorable."

"But then, you think he's adorable all the time," Natalie said. "And you know what, he feels the same way about you. He told me he is really going to miss you after this cruise."

I stared at Natalie a little uncomfortably. "I know, Nat, and that's exactly what I'm worried about."

"What do you mean?" she asked, puzzled.

"Well, what happens at the end of the trip? Do we all say goodbye and never see each other again? Mom says not to worry about that. But I can't stop thinking about it. I just can't." And with that, I burst into tears.

Chapter Ten

Natalie waited until my tears had stopped, then got a tissue and dried my cheeks. "Kari, there's a lecture going on in one of the small lounges in half an hour. I want to take you to it."

"What's it about?" I asked.

"It's called 'Overcoming Your Fears.' "

"A lecture on a cruise? It sounds boring."

"I'll bet you an ice-cream cone you'll want to stay."

I gave in. "OK, but you'd better get your ice-cream money out now. You're going to lose that bet."

"Come on," Natalie said. "I have a feeling this lecture is going to be crowded, and we want to get good seats."

Natalie was right about the crowds. When we got to the lounge, there were only a few seats left. We quickly grabbed two together. "Get me chocolate," I whispered as we sat down.

"Shhh," Natalie whispered back. "Give Dr. Bates a chance. She knows what she's talking about."

Dr. Bates turned out to be a gray-haired woman with a sympathetic face. She gained my trust immediately with her opening remarks. "We all have fears, even the bravest of us," she said. "Look around you. You're probably not the only one afraid of a particular something. Now, don't you feel better knowing you're not alone?"

The audience laughed, but she was right. I thought about my own fear of losing the people I loved. Everyone on the cruise had made a few new friends, and they all would be leaving them soon, just as I would.

"Most people," continued Dr. Bates, "try to hide their fears and end up feeling guilty about them. This is the worst way to deal with them. Get them out into the open! It's the only way you'll ever get over them. Now, I need a little participation from the group. Are a few of you willing to tell the rest of us your worst fear? Don't be shy. As I said, there are probably others in the room with the very same problems."

At first no one said a word. Then I felt Natalie pushing back her chair and standing up. "I'm really spooked by moths," she blurted out, and I could hear a giggle from the crowd.

Dr. Bates put up her hand to silence the laughter. "Please, this is a common problem. It could be spiders to some people, snakes or dogs to others. But it's really the same problem, so my answer might apply to many of you out there."

Natalie sat down quickly, and I could hear her breathing hard. I saw her hands shaking a bit. I wondered if that was because she'd stood up in front of all those people or because she was thinking of moths.

"With a fear like this, you might do a little work at the library. Study up on moths, get every book you can find. There are many species, and some are truly interesting. By getting to know them, you will eventually overcome your fear of them. You'll know when you're cured because instead of breaking out into a cold sweat when you see a moth, you'll be anxious to identify the species. This actually works."

I saw Natalie smile, and I knew she'd be at

the library as soon as she got home. "Forget the chocolate ice cream," I whispered to her, and she laughed.

Natalie had broken the ice with the crowd. After her confession many more people told of their fears. Each one was different, but nobody's was anything like mine. After a while I began to get impatient. I really wanted to get over my fear of being left alone, and it seemed as if Dr. Bates might be able to help me.

"If you want some advice, you're going to have to stand up and ask for it," Natalie whispered.

I looked at her for a moment. She was absolutely right. I let a few more people talk. Finally, I found the nerve to stand up and speak myself.

"Yes, dear?" Dr. Bates said.

"I—I'm afraid," I stuttered, "of losing the people I love."

"I'm glad you've admitted that," Dr. Bates said. "It's one of the most common fears I've come across. In fact, most people have it to some extent. You may have a particularly bad case of it. Let's face it, losing friends or family is hard. It hurts, and that's all there is to it. But there are so many things that hurt in life. It hurts to fall down, it hurts to stub your toe, it hurts to have a headache. We know these things will happen to all of us a few times, yet we don't walk around being afraid of them. They happen, and we accept them, knowing the pain will disappear with time.

"Why, then, are we so afraid of this particular kind of pain, emotional pain? It, like physical pain, will pass with time. Remembering this can really help us get over the fear of losing a loved one."

Well, it certainly wasn't an easy answer. I thought about all the things different people had said to me about my fear. Aunt Camille had talked about memories keeping me company. Mom had shown me the foolishness of missing out on good times just to avoid some bad ones. And Dr. Bates had told me to remember that pain passes. Maybe, just maybe, I had enough ways now to fight my fear. Maybe, at last, I could learn to control it.

"Thanks for bringing me, Natalie," I said. "You bet me an ice-cream cone I would want to stay. Well, I've stayed, so I guess I'll have to treat you. What flavor do you want?"

As it turned out, I had plenty of time to think things over that night. The ship tossed unrelentingly, and I wasn't able to shut my eyes for more than fifteen minutes at a time.

The advice I'd gotten from Aunt Camille, Mom, and Dr. Bates turned around and around in my head. I thought about how I'd felt after Dad had died. I'd been sure my heart would never be whole again, that my life was shattered forever. It still hurt to think of him, that was true, but I certainly wasn't shattered anymore. I was leading a happy, healthy, enjoyable life. There was no reason to think that I wouldn't get over Lisa leaving home or that I wouldn't stop missing Noah.

I thought about Mom and how much pain she must have experienced when Dad died. Now she'd met Ron. And for the first time, I realized just how wonderful that was. It didn't mean she'd stopped loving Dad. But she was letting go of her pain, the pain that had kept her from enjoying many of her old interests and hobbies. Mom had stopped being afraid of losing the people she loved, and now it was my turn to do the same.

Early in the morning the storm quieted down and passed. I was lulled into a calm, relaxed dream. I slept like a baby, without a worry in the world.

Chapter Eleven

I was awakened when the phone rang. It was Noah. His voice sounded lower, softer, less happy than usual. "Kari, can you spend the day with me in Nassau the way we did on Saint Thomas? I need to talk to you when there's no one else around."

"Sure," I said. "I think my mother probably wants to go off with Ron again. She hasn't said anything, but I bet she'll be happy that I have something to do."

"OK," he said. "I hear we'll be in Nassau only three hours because last night's storm put us way off schedule. Anyhow, maybe we can just walk around a little and look at the seashells. They have such beautiful ones there."

I figured I knew what was bothering Noah. The trouble between his parents must have come to a head. And from the way Noah sounded, the news wasn't good.

"I'll meet you at the tender," I said. "It's going to be a lovely day." I glanced at the porthole. The angry gray clouds had been replaced by fluffy white cotton ones. The waves were behaving themselves, gently lapping at the sides of the ship.

Noah didn't say anything about his parents all the way over to Nassau's Prince George Wharf. In fact, he hardly spoke at all. I watched him out of the corner of my eye as the tender slid away from the ship. His eyes were dull, and he had lost his smile. His hand felt cold when he slipped it into mine to guide me through the aisle of benches on the tender's deck.

The dock, like that at Saint Thomas, was full of taxis, shouting drivers, and tour guides, except it was even busier. Musicians welcomed us with calypso songs played on steel drums. Little kids wearing straw hats to large for them yelled out from under their brims, "Good deal, lady." They'd hold up shells or straw bags for me to look at. Constables in colorful uniforms tried to direct traffic, which included bikes, horse-drawn surreys, cars, and people. It had to be a frantic job.

Noah tugged on my hand, and together we maneuvered our way through the noisy throng. "I'm looking for another moped place, OK?" he asked.

"Sure. Is there any place special you want to visit?"

"You can't go home without seeing the horrible dungeons," he said. "My dad took me to them on our last trip."

We found a moped rental stand quickly. After the same warning about driving on the left side of the road, we set out, riding carefully around the outskirts of the straw market. "We'll come back here before we leave and pick up a few souvenirs, maybe a straw bag for you. And they have gorgeous conch shells," Noah called out to me.

We headed for the torture chambers and dungeons of Fort Charlotte. "The place was built by Lord Dunmore," Noah said when we reached the fort.

"I bet it's just like those old, scary movies," I said.

We parked our mopeds at the castle and joined the crowds of eager sightseers inside. Down we marched over crumbling stone steps to the castle's lowest level. It got darker and darker until the only light was from candles perched precariously on the edges of the steps. As my eyes became adjusted to the blackness, I could make out ancient rocks piled up against the walls. A musty smell filled my nostrils. I imagined that I was living in times long ago. I was sneaking into the dungeon to help the boy I loved escape from the cruel jailer. It was just as though I'd fallen into the pages of a novel.

But Noah and I didn't joke about the past I envisioned. He was very quiet, and I knew his mind was on much more serious matters. Without his laughter, the creepy dungeon was a little frightening, and I was glad when we left. Once we were outside, I gulped down the cool, fresh air.

"Let's head for the beach," Noah said as we got on our mopeds again. "They have the most amazing silver beaches here."

"Silver?"

"Yes. The sand is so pale, it shines like silver."

It was only a short ride to the beach, and we arrived in no time. I spread my sweater on the sand and sat down. Far out in the harbor I could see our ship waiting for us.

After a few moments of silence, Noah began to speak. "I never thought it would happen to me, to my family," he said. I didn't answer because I didn't think he actually expected me to. Poor Noah, he sat on the sand, hugging his knees to his chest as if they could comfort 'him. "They decided to get the divorce," he said. "They told us last night."

"It's all final?" I asked.

"Final." He scooped up a pile of sand and slowly let it sift through his fingers.

"You'll be going away to college next year, won't you, Noah? It won't be so bad then."

"We won't be together even on holidays," he answered glumly. "Nothing will ever be the same again. Nat will be going to Bryn Mawr; I'm off to Brown. The whole family's breaking up."

"You know," I said, piling sand on the hill he was building, "I've been feeling that way for a while now. When I was little, I thought our family would always be together, Lisa and me, my parents. Well, it hasn't turned out that way. But I'm trying not to have too many regrets. I'm trying to go with the changes and accept them." I found myself recounting my conversations with Aunt Camille, Mom, and Dr. Bates. "I feel different now, better. The past is over, and the future is ahead of me. Instead of feeling bad about things that have already happened, I'm trying to concentrate on the good things to come."

Noah was silent, considering my words. "I think what you've said is going to help me through a very difficult period." Suddenly he jumped up and pulled me to my feet. "Come on, let's walk."

We dusted the sand from our clothes. Noah walked toward the surf, stopping at the foamy edge of the water. He removed his shoes and wiggled his toes in the lapping swirls. Quickly I kicked off my sandals and joined him on the muddy sand. The water was not so cold as I'd expected. It felt wonderful on my hot feet.

Noah turned and smiled at me. "Kari," he said, facing me, "I'm lucky to have you. You're the best thing that ever happened to me. I know I'm not very good company today. But I just keep hoping I'll go back to that ship and my parents will tell me a miracle has happened—that they've decided to stay together and nothing will change. Everything will be the same as it always has been."

"You can't *make* people stay in love, Noah," I said softly, "even if they're your mother and father." We climbed a small hill of sand and perched ourselves on the top. "Noah,

103

let's try to find something positive about this change. Tell me, how will things be different for you now?"

He looked at me, puzzled. "Well, Dad will move out to California, and I'll have to travel back and forth from one coast to the other to see him."

"But, Noah, you say you love to travel. And maybe on one of your trips to the West Coast, you can stop by and visit me. Noah," I said softly, "it's not the end of the world."

He didn't answer back. We sat very close together on the sandy hill, our bowed heads touching. Silently we shared our painful, changing times.

After our serious time together on the beach, Noah and I opted for a change of mood. We turned in our mopeds and headed for the bustling, noisy market at Rawson Square. The cruise director had instructed everyone on the tender to bargain with the peddlers. "Don't pay the first amount they ask," he'd warned us. "They set a high price to begin with, expecting to be bargained down."

Noah and I approached the first straw-covered concession stand, and I began to look at the beautiful shell necklaces. There was one, particularly special, made of tiny pearly pink and creamy white shells. "Twenty dollars," the woman said, fanning her face with a straw fan.

"More like five dollars," I whispered to Noah, but loud enough so that the woman could hear. It was the first time I'd ever bargained, and I expected her to tell me to go somewhere else.

"OK," she said and smiled. "For five dollars it is yours."

I paid for the necklace, which she wrapped up in tissue paper, and I placed it carefully in my purse. "Now I want to buy myself a huge straw bag," I told Noah, "one I can drag down to the beach, big enough for towels and books and suntan lotion."

We passed several more booths, the owners calling to us with tempting offers. I headed for a stall crammed full of straw bags. I saw the perfect one immediately. A delicate design was woven into it using different colored straw. It was two different shades of burgundy with splashes of red for accent. It looked sturdy, too.

"Watch this!" I said to Noah as I edged up to the stand, making my way around other customers who were busy haggling.

The man started by asking twenty-five dollars. I touched the bag lovingly, and he cut the price to twenty. I turned and picked up a tiny shell to show I didn't want the bag at that price. The man said he'd take fifteen. Then I made my big move. "Let's go back to that other stand," I said loudly to Noah.

"It's yours for ten dollars," exclaimed the weary man. Excitedly I dug the money out of my purse and handed it to him. "Thank you," I said and smiled. "It's beautiful."

I placed my purse and my newly pur- chased necklace into the straw bag, and then we headed for the shell booths. I'd never seen such collections in my life. "Just wait until you see me do my stuff," Noah said and smiled.

"I'll be watching."

"Fifteen dollars," the man told Noah when he picked up a large conch shell. He looked as though he absolutely would not lower the price.

"Oh, that's too much," Noah told him firmly, but the tips of his ears were growing pink.

"Ten, then," the man said, picking up the most beautiful of the conches and placing it directly under Noah's nose.

"No more than five," Noah said bravely.

"You stab me where it hurts, young fellah," the man said, wiping the sweat from his forehead. "But since you buy it for this pretty lady, I accept your offer of five dollars."

Noah puffed with pride over his triumph. He stood there grinning while the man behind the counter wrapped the conch in old newspaper. I slipped it into my straw bag with all the rest of the things. "I'm beginning to feel like a back-packer," I said. "Noah, you were great."

"I thought so!" he said, throwing out his shoulders, and we both cracked up. We stopped at another booth, and after some more expert haggling, Noah purchased T-shirts for his sister and parents.

Too soon it was time to head back for the tender, and we took one long, last look at the straw market. "Thanks for the conch shell," I told Noah. "It's so beautiful. I'll put it on my bed table and think of you every time I look at it."

We pushed through the crowded area where the tender waited for us. The vendors along the seawall called out as we passed, shouting prices, trying to get us to buy just one more thing before we sailed away. "Oh, look at those shells." I grabbed Noah's arm. A row of conches was lined up on the wall, some of them still wet from the ocean. Most of them were much larger than the one in my bag. They were outstanding, and I couldn't help but comment on them.

"Right out of the sea," the man yelled to the onlookers who had lined up beside us. He held up one of the shells. "Two for a dollar."

Noah and I looked at each other. "Two for a dollar!" we both said at the same time. I started to laugh. "Oh, Noah, you sure can drive a hard bargain."

He grabbed two of the largest shells, the saltwater dripping from them. "I can't resist the price." He grinned.

The man didn't wrap the conches in old newspaper for us. But at that price, who could ask for old newspaper, too? We thrust the new shells into my straw bag along with our other purchases. Still laughing, we boarded the tender. That first man who had charged us a full five dollars for one shell must have come down to the seawall and bought them for two for a dollar, then raced back to his stand to give us a "good deal." If we'd had any guilty feelings about bargaining, they were gone by now.

Noah smiled and hugged me. It was good to see him laugh again.

Chapter Twelve

Noah walked me back to my cabin. I pushed open the door and called out to my mother, but she hadn't returned from Nassau yet. "I hope she didn't miss the last tender," I said nervously.

"She could have been on the same one as we were. It would have been easy to miss her in a crowd like that."

"It sure is nice to put this heavy bag down," I said. I laid the bag of treasures on the bedspread. One by one, I pulled out the conch shells. The five-dollar one, still wrapped in newspaper, was much smaller than the cheaper ones. We couldn't get over it.

Noah spotted my sketch pad on the table. It was flipped open to a drawing of people sitting on deck chairs on the International Deck.

"Hey, this is very good," he said, picking up the pad.

"Oh," I said, pleased but embarrassed. "Well, thank you. I don't usually let anyone see my sketch pad. Some of them aren't that good."

Noah flipped through the book slowly. He smiled.

"And who is this handsome guy?" He held up the drawing I'd done of him early in the trip.

"You really think he's good-looking?" I teased, sitting down on my bed.

"Definitely." He grinned, and then suddenly his smile started to fade. His eyes grew wider, and his mouth dropped open.

"What is it?" I cried. Noah looked as though he had seen a monster. "Noah, what's wrong!" I was scared now. Too scared to look behind me and too scared not to. Because whatever it might be, it was behind me!

Slowly I turned and followed his gaze. I jumped up, and my breathing froze for a moment when I saw it. There, right on the middle of my bed was a horrible creature. It was crawling sideways out of the largest conch shell. "It *is* a monster," I whispered, looking at its hooked tail and two large pinchers. I shuddered thinking about how close I'd been to those pinchers a moment ago. "Oh, Noah, it's horrible."

"It's only a hermit crab, though I've got to admit it's the biggest one I've ever seen. He must have been in that conch shell all the time."

"Oh, no!" I moaned. "All the time I was carrying those darn shells close to me, that thing was in one." Noah began to laugh, and I shot him a dirty look. "I think I'm going to be sick," I told him.

"You're not going to be sick."

"That's what you think! Noah, what are we going to do with it?" I asked. "I know one thing. If you don't catch it and get it out of this cabin, I'll never come back in here again. I'll sleep out on the deck for the rest of the cruise."

At that moment my mother pushed open the door. "Hi, kids." She gave us both a smile. Then her eyes went over to the bed, and she let out a shriek.

Ron, standing behind her, immediately dropped the straw bag and packages he was holding and put a comforting arm around Mom. "My gosh, it's a hermit crab," he said. "Poor thing. Don't be afraid, Judith, it's harmless. It's been making its home in that conch, and now it's being evicted."

My mother put her hand over her mouth, laughing at her own reaction. "You're right, it is rather sad. But it's so ugly."

"Not to another hermit crab," Ron said, his laughter filling the cabin.

"I'm Noah Walters," Noah said to Ron and held out his hand.

I couldn't believe it! Now, of all times he was introducing himself. Noah, Ron, and Mom started making small talk about Nassau, and I felt as though I wanted to scream. There was that totally awful creature in the middle of my bed, and the three of them were chatting like old friends at a reunion.

"OK," I said, "I'm going to go into that hallway, Noah Walters, and I'm staying there until you get rid of that sea monster. I really mean it."

I strode out, slamming the door, and stood in the hallway. I heard the three of them laughing and fooling around, trying to get the crab into one of my mother's shoe boxes. George, the steward, came by, and when I explained our trouble, he knocked on the cabin door and joined the hunting party. It took them almost ten minutes to catch that

112

thing. I waited in the corridor, feeling more and more like a coward. Finally Noah emerged from the cabin, the shoe box in his hands.

Carefully we walked down the corridors and then onto the open upper deck. Most of the passengers were getting ready for dinner, so the area was almost empty.

I ran over to the railing. "OK, Noah, dump him!"

"Don't you want just one more look at him to say goodbye?" Noah teased.

"If you don't—"

"OK, OK," he said and raised his arm in a beautiful, long pitch. The box flew out over the water, spun in the air, and then fell to the sea. We watched it hit the water, turn on its side, and bob up and down a short while. Soon, it had filled with water and disappeared into the dark waves.

"I hope it didn't get hurt." I sighed. "That was quite a drop."

"It was pretty large," Noah said, leaning over the rail. "I think it will survive until it can find itself another shell."

"Funny," I said. "It was in there all that time. I bet it was scary and strange for it when it found itself in the middle of a bed on a luxury cruise."

"I wish we could have kept it," Noah said wistfully. "It would have been fun to watch for a while like a pet."

"But it would've died."

"Oh, yeah, it would've been wrong to keep it. We did the best thing. It was the same with the little rabbit we found one summer."

"What rabbit?" I asked.

"Well, one vacation when we were up at my uncle's mountain cabin, a little wild rabbit got caught in one of my uncle's box traps. It was just a baby, so soft and cute, and I wanted to keep it. I cried like crazy when my uncle made me let it go. He told me that if I really loved it, I'd let it go so that it could be happy and free. You know, Kari, it was the hardest thing I'd ever had to do. But then, I was just a little kid."

I closed my eyes and wished I'd known Noah back then. I could almost see him with his tousled hair, holding a silky-coated rabbit. But life hadn't changed much since then. Both Noah and I were learning to let go of people we loved. And it was still the hardest thing we had to do.

Chapter Thirteen

Noah, Natalie, Lasse, and I climbed aboard a tender at nine the next morning. We had a very special day ahead of us, a stop on a spectacularly beautiful and uninhabited island. There was nothing on it, no historical sights to see, no shops to run into, just perfect white sand beaches and gentle waters filled with exotic fish. I couldn't wait. After all the running around we'd been doing, I thought it would be wonderful just to swim and lie on the beach.

The four of us had taken snorkeling lessons on the ship. We planned to spend some of the time using the snorkel masks and breathing pipes to spy on the magical underwater life of the sea creatures.

Our mood was bright. Everyone was filled with anticipation. I think Lasse must have been the most excited passenger on the whole ship. He'd told Natalie that he was planning to study underwater environments. This type of research would someday be his profession.

As I stepped off the tender, I said to Natalie, "Wow, this really is a paradise. It truly has to be one of the most beautiful spots on earth."

Natalie smiled. "You're absolutely right." She pretended nothing was bothering her, but her eyes were puffy. I could tell she'd been crying. That was the only thing to spoil the day.

We spent the early hours of the day in the water with our snorkel instructor. She gave us a short recap of our lesson on safety and how to use the equipment. She also lectured us on the different fish we might see through our masks. The water was unbelievably clear. The variety of fish was amazing.

After a few hours, the four of us shed our equipment and collapsed on the sand. "I would have died if that crab thing had been in the middle of my bed," Natalie said as we spread our beach towels on the sand.

"You only think it's ugly because you're not used to it," Noah said to her. "Now, other hermit crabs would have thought it was pretty good-looking, dancing sideways across the bedspread." He laughed. "If we could have kept it and gotten used to it, maybe we would have thought it was dashing and handsome."

"No way," Natalie told him.

"Right," I agreed with her.

"Hey," Noah said to me, "weren't you kind of repelled when you saw E.T. on the screen for the first few minutes of the movie?"

"You know, I think you're right," I said.

"And you fell in love with it later on."

"Oh, yes, I saw the movie three times."

I stretched out on the soft sand. The sun felt warm and comforting on my face. I looked out at the turquoise water of the sea. Everything was so perfect, like a dream come true. I thought about how I would have missed this day if I'd been silly enough to stay away from Noah the whole cruise. "I can't think of a thing I want right now," I said out loud to no one in particular.

"I can," Noah said. "Lunch. I'm starving."

"I just want to stay here and rest for a while," Natalie said.

"Look at that food line!" Lasse exclaimed, shading his eyes with his hand. "It looks like ants around a piece of candy."

"You two stay here," Noah said. "No need

for all of us to stand there in the sun. Lasse, come on, we'll get food for the four of us."

"Terrific!" I said, relieved that I wouldn't have to move a muscle. The sun certainly made me lazy.

Nat raised her head and looked over at the buffet table. The ship's calypso band started playing a bouncy, upbeat tune. Across from us a group had started a game of volleyball. "They're going to be in that line for half an hour at least," she said.

"Don't worry. Lasse will come running back to you as soon as possible," I teased her.

"Oh, yes," she shot back, "and my brother is probably heartbroken at having to spend a single moment away from you." She smiled, becoming more serious. "I'll tell you a secret, Kari. Noah thinks you're beautiful. He even told me he thinks he's in love with you. He says he's really learned a lot from you."

"Natalie," I confided, "I feel the same way about him. It's incredible to share so much with another person. And to think we didn't even know each other a week ago."

"Life is full of surprises," Natalie said bittersweetly.

We lay back again, enjoying the warmth of the sun and the soothing sounds of the waves

118

against the shore and the songs of the calypso band. I think I might even have fallen asleep because the next thing I knew, Noah was beside me.

"Madame, your feast awaits," he said and bowed. He was carrying two plates overflowing with goodies. Lasse was right behind him with two more plates.

After lunch Natalie and Lasse joined the volleyball game. Noah and I sat together watching the birds fly overhead. It was nice to be there and do nothing. Noah's silky hair fell over his forehead, and I leaned over and slid my finger under a reddish-blond lock.

He lay down and looked up at me. "You're wearing the necklace."

"I've never taken it off."

He reached up and touched the shining gold letters, letting each one slip through his fingers. I looked down at his face. He looked troubled and sad, and my heart went out to him. Slowly he stood. I watched him walk to the water's edge, his head down. He stood a moment on the wet sand before he dove in.

After a few minutes, I got up and strolled to the water. I jumped in and swam out to meet him. The water wasn't deep, and we stood for a moment, just looking into each other's eyes. Then Noah reached out and touched my face. With his other hand he encircled my waist. Then he bent and kissed me, a long, salty kiss.

"Did you love me from the very beginning?" he asked, slightly out of breath. "I don't think, Kari, that there was even one moment that I didn't love you."

I stared into his beautiful eyes, and, as seriously as I could, I said, "Noah, for me, it was a lot like with E.T. At first I was absolutely horrified. But then, slowly, I began to love you, no matter how awful and scary you looked."

I got the reaction I wanted, first a look of surprise, then a long, full laugh. His sadness was gone. Escaping from his grasp, I swam toward shore as fast as I could. He was inches from me. Quickly he closed the distance between us. Then he was beside me. He pulled me to him, and we kissed again.

I thought about Natalie's words. Noah said he'd learned a lot from me. I had to share my thoughts with him even if they made him sad. "Noah, you know what we have to do about our parents, don't you? In the last few weeks, I've really clung to my mom. But now I realize that she needs more than a daughter's love. She's met Ron, and he's become special to her. She needs him now. So I can make her life miserable by holding on to her too tightly."

Noah breathed out hard. "And you're saying that's what Nat and I have to do."

"That's right," I told him. "Because you love them and want the best for them, you'll have to let them go, just like that hermit crab or the wild rabbit."

"I guess I've known that all along," Noah said. He reached out and touched my cheek. "I just needed someone like you to tell me."

That evening we returned to the S.S. *Norway*, exhausted but happy, and ready for more celebrating. It was the night of the gala farewell dinner, and everyone would be dressed in their most elegant clothes. I wore my gold dress with a flowing black sash. Mom had on a simple but stunning lavender gown.

Together, we walked to the dining room. At the top of the red-carpeted stairs, we paused for a moment. I felt like a fairy princess. Ron, already seated at our table, spotted us. He stood up and gallantly raised his glass of water in honor of our arrival. My mother, delighted at his gesture, thanked him with a smile as she walked down the stairs toward him. I had to admit, in his black jacket, white

121

shirt, and bow tie, Ron was terribly good-looking.

The dinner, our last on the ship, was created for gourmets. I lost count of the courses. We had a wonderful time with our tablemates, toasting one another again and again. During the meal I began to feel sorry about losing my new friends. We'd all exchanged addresses, but I wondered how many of us would really keep in touch as we promised.

After dinner I had to dash off and meet Noah, Natalie, and Lasse to get ready for the big costume ball. I was glad to leave quickly, though. Long goodbyes make me sad.

We got together in the Lido Lounge after each of us had changed into our costumes. The crew had supplied us with three wet suits, and Natalie and I had finished her glittering mermaid costume. She looked terrific, her gold hair bouncing down her back, her crown shimmering in the lights. Mrs. Walters had made some final stitches in the sparkling gold- and silver-encrusted sheet, and it fit like a glove, or I should say, the scales of a fish.

The lounge started to fill with people in all kinds of outrageous outfits. There were cowboys, Dolly Partons, gorillas, clowns, angels, devils, ballerinas, and tramps. A terrific couple was dressed as Mae West and W.C. Fields. We were told to form a line in the hallway so that we could parade down the International Deck. A crew member walked down the line pinning numbers on everyone. We were number twenty-one. We started moving at last.

Boy, was there a crowd on the deck. I was glad I'd gotten over my fear of audiences; otherwise, I would have been a wreck. We three spear fishermen joined hands and bowed. Then Lasse went over to Natalie and scooped her up in his arms. The crowd roared with delight. Now all we had to do was wait for the prizes to be given out. As the master of ceremonies announced fourth, third, and second prizes, the tension mounted. Finally he said, "First prize goes to the most imaginative group, our mermaid and her captors."

The crowd cheered and clapped, and cameras flashed. We joined hands again and faced the audience. The cruise director held a gold statue in his hand. It was shaped like an old ship's figurehead, a woman with wings holding a wreath high. On the base were the words, "First Prize, S.S. *Norway*."

Natalie accepted the trophy for us. She looked over at me and smiled, her eyes sparkling. We'd done it! But there were four of us and only one trophy. What should we do?

"We could each keep it for two months," Noah suggested, "then pass it on."

"Sure," Lasse agreed.

"Let's give it to our mermaid first," I said.

"And I'll send it to Lasse," she agreed, looking up at him, smiling.

"He'll send it to me," Noah said quickly, "because by then, I think I might be able to hand-carry it to Kari."

"Wonderful," I said. "Then I'll send it back to Nat, and we'll start all over. How perfect. It will bind our friendships and hold together our great memories of the cruise."

"I've got a surprise for Kari," Noah said. "But it's something I'd like to share with all of you."

"Great," Lasse said. "I'd love to find out what it is as soon as I get out of this crazy costume. I feel as if they'll throw us overboard if we don't change soon."

"Let's meet in the Windjammer," Noah said, glancing at his watch. "It's twelve-thirty now. Be there by one."

Half an hour later I entered the Windjammer. It took me a minute to get used to the darkness, but finally I could see my three

124

friends over at a table near the stage. Noah waved me over excitedly.

"What's the surprise?" Nat asked. "I'm dying to know."

"Yeah," Lasse agreed, reaching out for her hand. "My mermaid is in a hurry because she has to return to the sea by two."

"You'll see in good time," Noah said. We ordered Cokes and talked about the next day, the day we would have to part. Our conversation slowed, a sadness filling the table.

"And now we have a pleasant surprise for you," the man on the tiny stage said. "We've asked one of our guests to sing for you. Welcome Noah Walters with a song he composed himself." Noah's guitar had been hidden behind the curtain, placed there hours before so that he could surprise us. The announcer smiled at him as he stepped up to the mike. The room fell silent. Noah picked up his guitar and began.

I've heard so many love songs,
A new one every day.
But I never dreamed I'd fall in love—
Then Kari walked my way.

Now I must write the songs myself,

A new one every day.
They tell you how I fell in love—
When Kari walked my way.

There were other verses, too. He sang them clearly, his voice like a ringing bell. He told of how he first saw me and fell in love with me, how our love grew. He told of how he'd never forget me, no matter how far apart we were.

I closed my eyes and cried.

Chapter Fourteen

We stood on the Pool Deck, Noah and I, watching the blinking stars. They were like tiny pinpricks in a black velvet cloth. "It's hard to believe we're almost in Miami now. When we wake up, we'll be there. The week went by so fast," I said.

"It wouldn't have mattered," he said softly, "if it had been a thousand weeks. It still would have gone by too fast."

"Uncle Craig and Aunt Camille will be waiting for us when we land in Los Angeles," I told him, sitting down on one of the reclining deck chairs. "They'll be so excited to hear all about our trip."

"And will you tell them about me?" Noah asked, sitting on the arm of the chair.

I laughed out loud. "Aunt Camille already knows about you!"

"You mean you called her?"

"Oh, no. She knew about you even before I did. I told her I thought I would never meet someone like you, someone who would love me as much as I loved him."

"And what did she say?"

"She said that when I least expected it, I'd turn a corner and there you'd be. Of course, she meant a corner of my life. She'll laugh when she hears it was a real corner."

A figure approached us. "Kari, is that you?" Mom asked.

"Yes. Oh, Mom, don't tell me it's time to go!"

"I'm afraid it's two-thirty already, and we have to have all our bags packed and placed outside our cabin by four in the morning."

"It can't be," I said and moaned. "Just give me five minutes more," I pleaded. "I'll pack everything in a hurry and be done before you know it."

She reached out her hand to Noah. "In case we don't see each other again, good luck, Noah."

He took her hand. "Thank you, Mrs. Langtree, but I'm pretty sure I'll be stopping by Los Angeles for a visit."

My mother disappeared down the stairs,

and I sat back again on the chair. "I'll have my own room for the first time in my life," I told Noah.

"That's great," he answered.

"You know, for once, I think it might be. When I get back, I'm going to redecorate."

He leaned over, put his arms around me, and kissed me. After a moment he said, "Remember, Kari, someday you'll open your front door, and I'll walk in with our trophy."

"That's a promise?"

"A solemn oath," he answered.

I looked down at my watch. "It's time for me to go." I stood up suddenly.

Noah was still sitting on the arm of my chair, and without my weight to counterbalance it, the seat tipped down, dumping him to the deck. We both laughed as he struggled to his feet. He stood up and dusted off his pants.

"I guess I can say now that I really fell for you," he said, kissing me on the cheek. His mouth found mine, and we kissed for the last time. Slowly we walked back to our cabins. It was over.

Even before I opened my eyes Saturday morning at six-thirty, I knew there was some kind of strange movement outside our portholes. I stood up and yawned. We'd only gotten a few hours of sleep after the packing. I climbed up on the bed, parted the drapes, and peeked out the porthole. "We're surrounded by all kinds of ships!" I exclaimed.

My mother came running out of the bathroom and climbed up on her own bed to see. Slowly our floating hotel made its way into the harbor. From far off, we could hear foghorns of other ships sliding into the harbor. The tall buildings of Miami stood like soldiers in a line along the edges of the beach.

"When I was a little girl," my mother said, "we used to use the expression 'Waiting for your ship to come in.' I always thought it meant a real ship loaded down with gold and lace and jewels. It wasn't until I was older that I realized it meant good fortune."

She looked over at me. "It was nice last week at the Omni Hotel watching the *Norway* sail in."

"I guess not many people can say they've watched their ship come in," I said and laughed.

"Not many," she said, hugging me to her. Suddenly she leaned over and gave me a smart smack on my rear. "Let's move it, Kari. We'll miss our breakfast." She peeked out into the hall. "The luggage is gone. All we have to take are our carry-on bags. I wonder how long it will take to go through customs."

"I asked George yesterday," I told her. "He said about two hours."

At seven-thirty we took one last look around our cabin, then went down to breakfast. Noah and Natalie waved to me from their table. Everyone was anxious to eat fast and hurry through customs. Ron hadn't taken the time for breakfast, my mother told me. He had to catch a plane into Chicago for a photographer's convention. My mother and I didn't have to hurry. Our plane didn't depart for another four hours, so we could leave at a leisurely pace and stay out of the way of the passengers who had to make plane or train connections.

When we finally reached the International Deck, we found it was swarming with people. We chose to sit in the Checkers lounge, where we just relaxed and listened to the others saying goodbye. Suddenly over the loudspeaker came the words, "Customs has now cleared the ship. You may leave at this time. We hope you had an enjoyable cruise with us and that you'll come visit us again. Have a safe trip home and in Norwegian tradition, *Velkommen Tilbake!*"

Most of the crowd jumped up, anxious to be on their way. My mother and I sat quietly, watching them depart. "It's better to sit here in these comfortable chairs and let the crowds go than push and shove and then sit in the airport," she told me.

After a while I walked out to the deck and watched the long line of passengers down below going through the process of claiming their baggage. There were dozens of taxis and buses lined up beside our ship, hundreds of people scurrying in all different directions.

An hour passed, and my mother appeared at my side. "I guess we'd better be going now," she said, "before they carry us off." We wound our way down the ramp toward the clusters of leftover baggage. There, we found ours all neatly stacked together. I leaned over to pick up a suitcase, and when I stood up, there was Noah standing on the curb beside two taxis. Nat was there, too, kissing her father goodbye. I could tell even from that far away she was crying.

Noah had told me his father was flying to New York to visit one of his editors and would spend Christmas week there. Noah, Natalie, and Mrs. Walters planned to stay in Miami for Christmas week and fly back to Pennsylvania later.

Mr. Walters hugged his daughter. Then he leaned over and gave his wife a long hug and kissed her, too. He turned to Noah and extended his hand. Noah's hand shot out and clasped his father's. Suddenly Noah's father threw his arms around his son. For one more moment, they held on to each other. Then they broke apart, and Mr. Walters stepped into one of the cabs. Instantly he wound down one of the back windows so that he could wave goodbye just one more time.

"Are you coming, Kari?" my mother called to me, walking toward the curb and the parade of taxis, carrying her share of the luggage.

At that moment Noah looked up and saw me. His face broke into a slow smile, and then Nat saw me, too. She held up an object wrapped in tissue, our special trophy. "Remember, Kari, you'll get your turn!" she shouted.

"Don't forget to send it to Lasse," I called back to her.

Noah touched his lips and then raised his

hand to throw a silent, invisible kiss to me. I caught it in midair and pressed it to my lips.

"Goodbye, Prince Andrew," I whispered. "Goodbye, Noah!"

Noah and Natalie crowded into a taxi, and it pulled away from the curb quickly. I could see their faces pressed against the back window, their hands still waving. I touched the chain around my neck, and I felt the word "love" dangling from the tiny links of gold.

It was my turn now to climb into a cab, and I settled back, having no one left to wave to. Finally I turned back and waved at my beautiful ship. Would the S.S. *Norway* miss Nat and Lasse, Noah and me? Would the crew ever talk about the mermaid and three fishermen who had won first prize for their costumes? Would they ever remember a certain boy who had sung in the Windjammer one night and the girl who sat at the table and cried?

"We're on our way home at last," my mother said, breaking the spell. "Are you glad?"

"In a way," I told her.

With the heat of Miami blowing through the open cab windows, it was hard to believe that Christmas was only a day away. "Air conditioning's broken down," the driver apologized.

It was OK with me. I was glad the windows were open because I could hear the lively city noises around us, the tinkling of the Christmas bells on the street posts, and the bustle of late shoppers. I could even smell the pine of the large green wreaths on the streetlights. It would be warm in California, too, but not quite so warm or humid.

"I wonder if Lisa missed me?"

"You know she did," my mother answered. "And we have so much to tell your aunt and uncle."

I thought again of Noah and Natalie. They would be OK, and so would I. After all, we had our memories.

We hope you enjoyed reading this book. All the titles currently available in the Sweet Dreams series are listed on the next two pages. Ask for them in your local bookshop or newsagent. Two new titles are published each month.

If you would like to know more about Sweet Dreams, or if you have difficulty obtaining any of the books locally, or if you would like to tell us what you think of the series, write to:—

United Kingdom	Australia
Kim Prior,	Sally Porter,
Corgi Books,	Corgi and
Century House,	Bantam Books,
61-63 Uxbridge Road,	26 Harley Crescent,
London W5 5SA,	Condell Park 220,
England	N.S.W., Australia

17850 4	THE TRUTH ABOUT ME AND BOBBY V (41)	Janetta Johns
17851 2	THE PERFECT MATCH (42)	Marian Woodruff
17850 2	TENDER LOVING CARE (43)	Anne Park
17853 9	LONG DISTANCE LOVE (44)	Jesse Dukore
17069 4	DREAM PROM (45)	Margaret Burman
17070 8	ON THIN ICE (46)	Jocelyn Saal
17071 6	TE AMO MEANS I LOVE YOU (47)	Deborah Kent
17072 4	DIAL L FOR LOVE (48)	Marian Woodruff
17073 2	TOO MUCH TO LOSE (49)	Suzanne Rand
17074 0	LIGHTS, CAMERA, LOVE (50)	Gailanne Maravel
17075 9	MAGIC MOMENTS (51)	Debra Spector
17076 7	LOVE NOTES (52)	Joanna Campbell
17087 2	GHOST OF A CHANCE (53)	Janet Quin-Harkin
17088 0	I CAN'T FORGET YOU (54)	Lois I. Fisher
17089 9	SPOTLIGHT ON LOVE (55)	Nancy Pines
17090 2	CAMPFIRE NIGHTS (56)	Dale Cowan
17871 7	ON HER OWN (57)	Suzanne Rand
17872 5	RHYTHM OF LOVE (58)	Stephanie Foster
17873 3	PLEASE SAY YES (59)	Alice Owen Crawford
17874 1	SUMMER BREEZES (60)	Susan Blake
17875 X	EXCHANGE OF HEARTS (61)	Janet Quin-Harkin
17876 8	JUST LIKE THE MOVIES (62)	Suzanne Rand
24150 8	KISS ME, CREEP (63)	Marian Woodruff
24151 6	LOVE IN THE FAST LANE (64)	Rosemary Vernon
24152 4	THE TWO OF US (65)	Janet Quin-Harkin
24153 2	LOVE TIMES TWO (66)	Stephanie Foster
24180 X	I BELIEVE IN YOU (67)	Barbara Conklin
24181 8	LOVEBIRDS (68)	Janet Quin-Harkin
24254 7	CALL ME BEAUTIFUL (69)	Shannon Blair
24255 5	SPECIAL SOMEONE (70)	Terri Fields
24355 1	TOO MANY BOYS (71)	Celia Dickenson

NON-FICTION TITLES

17859 8	THE SWEET DREAMS BEAUTIFUL HAIR BOOK	Courtney DeWitt
17838 5	THE LOVE BOOK	Deidre Laiken and Alan Schneider
17845 8	THE BODY BOOK	Deidre Laiken and Alan Schneider
17077 5	HOW TO TALK TO BOYS AND OTHER IMPORTANT PEOPLE	Catherine Winters